The
Turnabout Shop

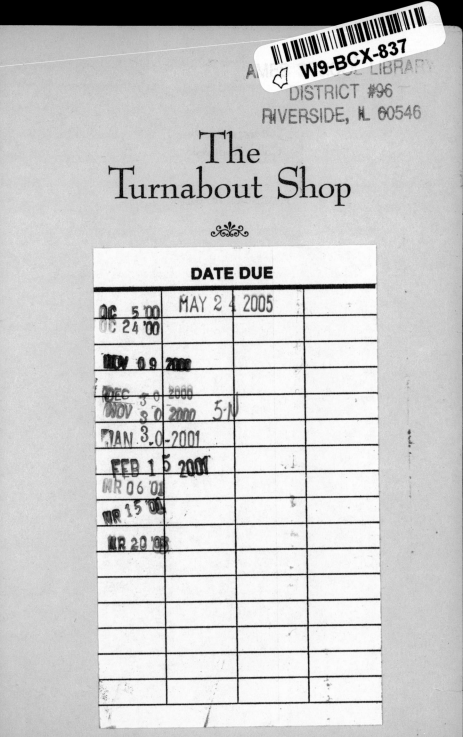

Other Books by
Colby Rodowsky

REMEMBERING MOG

The Turnabout Shop

❧

COLBY RODOWSKY

HarperTrophy®
A Division of HarperCollinsPublishers

HarperTrophy® is a registered trademark of HarperCollins Publishers, Inc.

The Turnabout Shop
Copyright © 1998 by Colby Rodowsky

For information address HarperCollins Children's Books, a division of
HarperCollins Publishers, 1350 Avenue of the Americas, New York, NY 10019.

Library of Congress Cataloging-in-Publication Data
Rodowsky, Colby F.
    The Turnabout Shop / Colby Rodowsky.
        p.   cm.
    Summary: In "conversations" with her dead mother, fifth-grader Livvy
records her adjustment to living in Baltimore with a woman she had never met, and
comes to see the wisdom of her mother's choice as she gets to know the woman's
large, loving family.
    ISBN 0-380-73192-4 (pbk.)
    [1. Mothers and daughters—Fiction. 2. Death—Fiction. 3. Grief—Fiction.
4. Orphans—Fiction.] I. Title.
PZ7.R6185Tu   1998   97-33229
[Fic]—dc21   CIP

First HarperTrophy edition, 2000
❖
Visit us on the World Wide Web!
www.harperchildrens.com

To
Margaret Jones
Pedro Ramos
Virginia Rodowsky
· Anna Jones

The Turnabout Shop

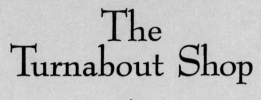

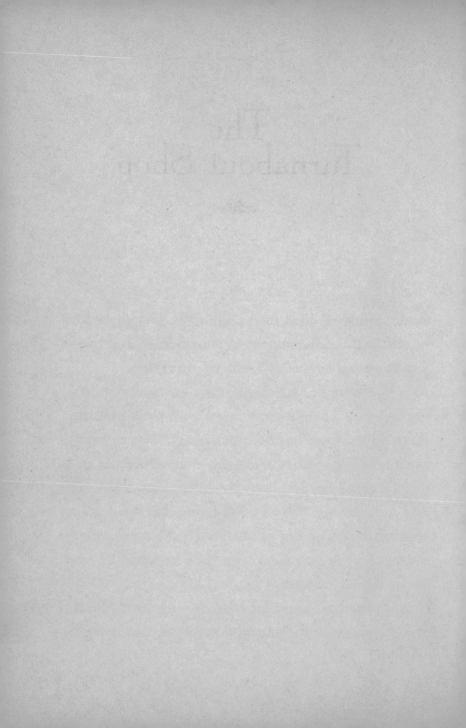

Fred, the lawyer, took me to Baltimore. Before we left, he said he was delivering me to Jessie Barnes, as if I were a package and he the UPS man or something.

We went on the Metroliner, which cost more than the regular train but got there faster, and the whole trip down from New York he kept saying, "Not to worry, not to worry," and rubbing his fingers together in a papery-sounding way. After a while, I tuned him out and concentrated instead on thinking that this was the fourteenth-saddest day of my life. The first was the day my mother, Althea, died, and the rest were the next twelve days in between.

From then till now, I'd been staying with Althea's friends Joannie and Pete and their twins, and trying to pretend I wasn't totally squishing everybody out of their broom closet of an apartment on Sixty-third Street. Joannie is a therapist. Every night, after the twins were in bed, she'd hand me paper and pastels and tell me to draw my feelings. And every night, when I'd crisscrossed the page in black, she'd give me a hug—and another piece of paper.

This morning, when I was getting ready to leave, she and Pete presented me with an Earth Day tote bag filled with notebooks and pens. "No matter what happens, Livvy," she said, "just remember to write it out."

"Not to worry," Fred said again as the train lurched to a stop, and right then I decided I would write it out *to Althea*—not on paper, though, but only in my head. It would be a kind of endless letter to my mother, because the way I figured it, that'd be the only way I could survive. And I had to survive. On account of one of the last things Althea said to me was "No matter what happens, you're a survivor, Ann Olivia Lyons. And don't you forget it."

1

Do you remember that, Althea? Do you remember? It was the day I came home from school and Fred was there, which wasn't all that odd in itself. I mean, through the years I'd gotten used to Fred, because of him being the one who managed your parents' trust fund and got to say, when times were tough, whether you could have more money or not. Because of him being the one who hired the nurses when you got sick.

What *was* odd that particular day was that Fred was there and you were gone. And so were the nurses in the white polyester pantsuits, who all looked alike and walked on cushiony feet and said, "Let your mother rest" and "Stay off the bed," even when you patted the place beside you and said, "Hop up here, Mousekin."

"Where's Althea?" I said, coming in the door and dropping my backpack.

"Your mother is in the hospital, Livvy. She took a turn for the worse this morning and the doctor thought it would be a good idea. We've got some interim arrangements set up—you'll be staying with Joannie and Pete Bullington until this crisis has passed."

And the weird thing was that the whole time he was talking, I could almost see you standing behind him, puffing out your cheeks and talking in your Fred voice, the way you did sometimes when we were alone.

"When will she be home?" I asked. "How soon?"

"I don't know," he said, making his hands into a steeple and staring down into it. "Very soon, I hope. But it depends, of course. It depends." He cleared his throat and pulled a piece of paper out of his pocket, as if he had to remind himself what to say next. "Now, if you'll just get some clothes together, and your schoolbooks, too, I'll take you to the hospital to see your mother on our way to the Bullingtons'."

I'd never been to a hospital before, and deep down I thought it'd be like it was in *Madeline*—you know, that book we read about a million times when I was little—and that you'd be standing on the bed showing off a scar and surrounded by a roomful of toys. And that there'd be a crack on the ceiling in the shape of a rabbit. It wasn't like that, though. If anything, you looked worse than you had at home and held tight to my hand and kissed my fingers one at a time with lips that were dry and cool. Remember, Althea? That's when you said it. When you caught me by the arm and were suddenly stronger than I thought it was possible for you to be and you said, "No matter what happens, you're a survivor, Ann Olivia Lyons. And don't you forget it."

The next day at school, when I stopped to sharpen my pencil, I heard Ms. Strapensky talking to the librarian in a whispery voice and nodding in my direction and saying, "The situation is positively Dickensian."

After supper, when I was helping Joannie give the twins a bath, I asked her what "Dickensian" meant, and she said, "Oh, you know, Livvy. It has to do with the writer Dickens, and it's usually something sad and sentimental and filled with orphans."

That night it happened. I heard the phone ring very late and I knew. Even before Joannie came in and held me tight and told me, I knew.

There's something I need to understand, Althea. I mean, where *are* you? Now. Oh, I know all about the burial next to your parents someplace outside the city, up on a hill, and how you told Fred beforehand not to let me go. And how I went off instead to Gretchen's loft with a bunch of your friends for what they called a Celebration of Althea's Life. You'd've liked it, because what it was was a party, with everybody sitting around on the floor talking about you: about how much fun you'd always been and how you loved the carousel in Central Park and riding the Staten Island ferry and smooshing your face up against the fish tank in the pet shop on Third Avenue.

They talked about how you wanted to be a writer and worked in a bunch of bookstores around town and went to readings in coffeehouses and sometimes took writing courses that you didn't always finish. And how you were finally making progress on a novel when you got sick.

"But Livvy was her magnum opus," someone said.

"I was?" I said, not at all sure what a magnum opus was.

"Her greatest work. You were Althea's greatest work," Joannie said.

And then everybody looked at me as if I were a trained seal and they were waiting for me to perform.

"Hear! Hear!" said Pete, holding up his glass.

"Hear! Hear!" they all said together.

I scrunched back against the wall and tried to turn invisible. I looked up at a shiny giant bagel suspended from the ceiling and hoped that it wasn't Gretchen's magnum opus.

After a while, they all started talking about openings and galleries and readings. They seemed to have forgotten about you, and me too, so I went off to Gretchen's bathroom and sat on the floor and cried and wiped my eyes on the edge of the shower curtain and stayed there till Joannie knocked on the door and said it was time to go.

That's why I really need to know where you are now. The *you*ness of you. Are you watching me from around every corner? Or maybe a star?

Are you a star, Althea?

Another thing I need to know is just who is Jessie Barnes? I mean, there I was on the train with Fred the lawyer on my way to Baltimore to live with Jessie Barnes, and I didn't even know who she was.

"A friend of your mother's," Fred said. "From her college days."

You could have *told* me, Althea. I can think of about a hundred times when you could have told me. Like when the nurses first came and were creeping around the apartment bringing you pills in little paper cups and squishy invalid meals. You could have pulled me up on the bed beside you and put on your serious face and said, "Now, look, Livvy, I want you to know that if anything ever happens to me, you'll be going to stay with my best of all possible friends—the exciting and fabulous Jessie Barnes."

Thirty-three words. You could have said them.

Or before that: the last time we went to the museum to see the mummies and you made your body go all stiff and did the mummy-walk around the gallery. You could have slipped it in there.

Or before that. The time when I was nine and we watched that incredibly sad movie on television about a woman who knew she was dying and made arrangements for what to do with her children. And I asked you straight out, "What if that happens to us?"

"It's not going to happen. It wouldn't dare," you said, getting up and dancing around the living room, stomping your feet and beckoning me to join you. "Come on, Livvy," I remember you saying. "Come and join the dance." But for once I didn't get up and follow you. For once I stayed put, digging my feet in and locking my hands behind my back. "What if, Althea. Just tell me what if."

"Your mother gave this a lot of thought," said Fred. "She considered all the possibilities and weighed the pros and cons to find just the right person to act as your guardian. Because of there being no family."

No family . . . no family . . . no family. The words rattled in my head and I thought of the bedtime stories you used to tell me. Not the regular kind with Cinderella or the three bears, but real-life stories of how you dropped out of college and traveled some and wandered some, waiting tables and singing in small cafés and reading poetry out loud. And how when you were in New Mexico you had a baby. Me.

"Didn't I have a father?" I always asked.

"Everyone has a father, Livvy," you always answered, pushing the hair out of my eyes and kissing me on the nose before you went on. "You just don't have one now, because I never saw fit to mention that you were on the way before he headed west, California-bound."

"And we came back here?" I'd prompt, wanting to get to the moving-to-New-York part.

"We came back here and became a twosome, a duo, a matched pair," you would sing out, something about your voice making me happy and sad, both at the same time.

"Why didn't she tell me what would happen to me if anything happened to her?" I asked Fred, my voice sounding thin and quivery.

"She wanted to, Livvy, but she could never find the words. And I think that up until the end, Althea still thought she would get well. Anyway, she finally decided that Jessie Barnes, as her most sensible friend, was the one to take care of you," he said.

Sensible, Althea? Since when were you into *sensible*?

No wonder I never heard of Jessie Barnes. Do you know what sensible is? It's clunky shoes and pulled-back hair and yucky vanilla pudding. It's going to bed early and getting up early and never ever going up on the roof in the middle of the night to see the moon.

Is that what you want for me? Is it, Althea? Is it?

And besides all that, I have one more question. *What's wrong with Jessie Barnes?* That she said yes to taking me, I mean. Just wham, bam, out of the blue—instant kid. What's wrong with her, Althea? What's wrong with her?

2

And another thing. If you'd told me about Jessie Barnes, then you could have shown me a picture of her, and Fred and I would have known what to expect as we started up the stairs of the train station in Baltimore.

We almost didn't get there, though, because partway to the top my legs gave out. Just stopped, as if I were a marionette and someone forgot to pull the leg strings. I sat down on the step, holding tight to the railing, while people stepped around me and over me and banged me with their boxes and bags.

"Are you all right?" Fred asked after he'd figured out I wasn't behind him anymore and came back.

"Uh-huh," I mumbled, my face twitching with all the things I wanted to say but couldn't. Like: "Why'd I have to come here? Why couldn't I have stayed with Joannie and Pete? Or even with Gretchen and the giant bagel?"

"Why couldn't Althea have stayed with me?"

"Let's go, Livvy," said Fred, balancing my suitcase on the edge of the step and reaching to help me up. "Let's see if we can find Ms. Barnes."

"Look for the feet, then," I said, grabbing my tote bag and my knapsack and scrambling after him.

"The what?"

"The feet—for the big, clunky, sensible Jessie Barnes shoes," I sort of mumbled, but Fred was already way in front, hurrying up the stairs.

"She said she'd be waiting at the Information Desk," he said when I caught up with him at the top.

Together we moved into the waiting room, looking out over the crowd until we saw the woman. Way to go, Althea, I thought as I stared at her. She was dressed in jeans and a silver-studded shirt. A red cape that seemed to swoop and swirl even when she was standing still was thrown over her shoulders. And on her feet she wore awesome snakeskin boots with curling toes. But as I watched, she suddenly waved to a man at the far end of the station and hurried to meet him.

The real Jessie Barnes waited behind her.

You could have warned me, Althea. You could have told me she was a moth instead of a butterfly. That she was little and that she'd come all done up in khaki—raincoat, rainhat, and a drippy, pointy khaki umbrella that was making a puddle on the floor next to the Information Desk.

The moth-woman turned and saw us and came toward us. "I'm Jessie," she said. "And you must be Fred—and Livvy. I'm glad to meet you." She took my hand and held it, sort of caught between both of hers. "I'm very sorry about your mother. Althea was always—well, special, and it must—you must—" She stopped, then started up again all in a rush. "I just want you to know that I'll do my best for you, Livvy. That I'll be here for you."

She let go of my hand and I took a step back, and then another and another, and would have kept going, down the steps and along the tracks, all the way to New York, if Fred hadn't reached out and caught me, pulling me forward.

"Let's have something to eat and get acquainted," he said. And the next thing I knew, the three of us were in the station restaurant, with menus the size of poster boards, and Fred and Jessie Barnes talking about pasta and chicken and seafood, and me feeling like I was going to throw up.

"What would you like, Livvy?" asked Fred.

"I don't know," I said.

"Chicken?" said Jessie Barnes. "Or how about a crab cake? We're pretty well known for our crab cakes here in Maryland."

"Just a hamburger, I guess."

"Bor-ing," I seemed to hear you say. *"Bor-ing, bor-ing, bor-ing,"* the way you did that time we went to the Japanese restaurant and I wanted peanut butter and jelly instead of sushi. Remember, Althea? And the time at Mamma Mia's when I asked the waitress if they had SpaghettiOs and you tried to pretend you didn't know me, that I was just some kid who'd wandered in off the street and sat at your table. Remember?

When the food came, I picked at my roll and listened as Fred and Jessie Barnes talked about schools and trust funds and a bunch of other things that seemed to be about someone else and not have anything to do with me at all. Afterward we went back out into the station, to the spot next to the Information Desk where we had started.

"Well," said Jessie, "have a good trip back. And don't worry about Livvy and me. We'll be fine."

Fred put my suitcase on the floor, nudging it with his foot in the direction of Jessie Barnes. He held out his hand to me. And the totally weird thing was that seeing him push at my bag like that made me realize for the very first time that he was leaving and I was staying.

That you weren't back in New York waiting for me.

That now it really truly was just me and Jessie Barnes.

Me and Jessie Barnes in her car going home. Me and Jessie Barnes on opposite sides of the front seat with a big fat silence crowding in between.

Okay, Althea, okay. Jessie Barnes and I. But no matter how I say it, it was still the two of us, alone in the car with the rain sloshing down around us and not a single thing in the world to say.

"I hope you're going to like Baltimore," she said after what seemed like ages.

I'm not going to like it at all, I wanted to shout back at her. Same as I'm not going to like having to live with you and see you every day and sleep in your house when I don't even *know* you—even on my birthday—and have you sign the papers from whatever weirdo school I'm going to have to go to when they say, "Take this home for your parents to sign." Because you're not my parents. You're not Althea.

I didn't, though. Say any of that, I mean. Because I was pretty sure it'd just be a mouthful of what you used to call wanton words. And I remember how, to your way of thinking, Althea, wanton words ranked right up there with telling lies and not pooper-scooping when you walked a dog.

17

"I guess it'll be okay," I said instead. I wrapped my arms around my backpack and held it tight, looking out the window and wondering if all of Baltimore looked like the rainy, dreary, boring part we were going through now.

After a while, we pulled up in front of a tall city house.

"I'll leave the car out here tonight," said Jessie. "Though usually I park around back and go in and out by way of the fire escape."

We grabbed my stuff and ran for the house, stopping when we got to the vestibule and shaking like big wet dogs. "We're on the second floor," she said, unlocking the outside door and holding it open for me. I started up the stairs and stopped, turning to watch as the door swung shut behind us.

On Jessie Barnes and me.

3

You know something, Althea? Jessie Barnes's apartment is filled with a bunch of really old stuff. Not tattery old, but old-old. As in antiques. And you know what else? She and her mother, Ivy, own a store together called The Turnabout Shop, where they sell antiques and collectibles and things.

She told me all this last night when we got back from the train station. The only trouble was that I couldn't think of anything to answer back to what she was telling me. And she couldn't think of anything to add to what I wasn't saying. So after that we just sat there, staring at the news on television, until the reporter's voice started sounding muffled and far away and my eyes kept closing and I had to blink them and pinch my arms to wake myself up.

"Come along, Livvy," said Jessie Barnes. "Why don't you go to bed." She steered me down the hall to my room and stood for a minute, looking puzzled, as if there was something more she was supposed to do, only she couldn't remember what it was.

"Well," she said finally, "the blue towel on the back of the bathroom door is yours, and there's toothpaste in the medicine chest. Be sure and call me if you need anything. And have a good night."

I washed my face and brushed my teeth, put on my nightshirt, and slithered down between covers that were stiff and cold, positive that I'd never in a million years get to sleep. And the next thing I knew, it was morning and the girl and the rabbit were looking at me.

You'd have freaked out, Althea. I mean, they weren't real or anything, just a picture in an old-timey frame of an incredibly nerdy girl holding a fat white rabbit. But still, they were on the wall opposite the bed and *staring straight at me.* I stared back at them until I was pretty sure they would have blinked—if they could have blinked—and then went on to examine the rest of the room, which I'd been too tired to notice much the night before.

It was okay, I guess, but it wasn't *mine.* And it never

would be, not in a million years. I was lying in a spool bed with spindles that squeaked when I twisted them and a patchwork quilt. I noticed dried flowers in a pitcher on the dresser and a little rocking chair next to the window. And the only thing that kept the room from looking like something in a museum was my open suitcase with my clothes spilling onto the floor.

I thought about all my books, which Fred had promised to send from New York, and wondered where I would put them. I remembered my Narnia poster with the picture of Aslan the lion on it and tried to decide where to hang it. But all I could see were that girl and that rabbit, staring at me again. I stuck my tongue out at them, then eased my way out of bed and across the room, inching the door open and stepping out into the hall.

I could tell by the way the silence sort of wrapped around me that the apartment was empty, and when I got to the kitchen I found a note propped up on the table. "Gone for bagels. Be right back. Jessie."

As soon as I read it, I hurried down the hall, figuring I could use this time to check out the apartment without Jessie Barnes watching me look at it. There was even more old-fashioned stuff in the living room than I remembered: candles in brass holders, a funny painted chest with the TV and VCR hidden inside, and one of those alphabet sampler things hanging on the wall between the windows.

I moved on to her bedroom, flipping through the papers on the dresser, peering at the snapshots stuck all around the mirror. I picked up a picture in a silver frame of a bunch of people I'd never seen before, except for Jessie Barnes, who was standing in the middle of the back row next to a man with blond hair who had his arm around her shoulder. Who was he? Where was he now?

I checked the row of sensible shoes in the closet. I stopped for a minute to try out the exercise step thing, going up and down, up and down, and then went over to the bedside table. Remember what you told me once, Althea? About how if you really want to know someone, see what books they have on their bedside table. Okay. Jessie Barnes had two mysteries, a book about shells, a dictionary, and a magazine called *Antiques*. Underneath all that, though, were two big fat books with about a hundred little slips of paper marking about a hundred pages: *You and Your Foster Child* and *Adopting the Older Child*.

Right away my hands started to sweat, my knees to shake. I mean, part of me wanted to sit down and read what she had read, and part of me wanted to drop those books right out the window. Before I could decide which

I wanted to do more, I heard a key in the lock of the kitchen door and I turned and flew out of there.

"Good morning," said Jessie Barnes when I wandered into the kitchen a minute later, trying to pretend I wasn't out of breath. "I hope you found my note. I just ran down to get some bagels. There's sunflower and poppy and a couple of plain, in case you'd rather, so just help yourself." She dropped the bag on the counter and opened the refrigerator, taking out orange juice, cream cheese, and a jar of jam. Then she turned to ask, "Did you sleep well?"

"Oh yes. Fine, thanks," I said, and realized we'd hit one of those stuck places in the conversation again. I wondered if there was anything in one of her books that said what to do about that.

"Later on we'll go to—"

"What about that rabbit—"

We both started to speak at the same time, and both stopped at the same time.

"Sorry," we both said together. Then we waited, each nodding to the other, till Jessie Barnes finally shrugged and said, "Okay, me first. Later on we'll go to the store and you can tell me what kind of cereal you prefer, what you like for lunch. Then we'll go on to The Turnabout Shop. Now it's your turn."

23

"I was just going to ask about the rabbit. You know, the fat one in the picture."

"He's wonderful, isn't he?" she said, which wasn't exactly what I'd been thinking. She filled the kettle and put it on the stove before going on. "I was taken with that rabbit, and the girl, too, when someone brought the picture into the shop for us to sell, and I ended up buying it myself and bringing it home. That's the trouble with being in the business I'm in—I'm forever finding things I can't live without. But it works both ways, because when I no longer have room for something, or find I *can* live without it, I just recycle it back through The Turnabout Shop."

The whole time I was eating, I thought about what it would be like if I could recycle the parts of my life I didn't like back in to The Turnabout Shop, trading Jessie Barnes for you, Althea, Baltimore for New York, this sit-on-the-furniture apartment for our comfortable sit-on-the-floor one. I swallowed hard and looked down at the piece of sunflower bagel left on my plate, and knew that that worked only for chairs and tables and pictures of nerdy girls and large white rabbits.

When we had finished eating, Jessie got up to clear the table. "I'll clean up in here while you take your shower and get dressed," she said. "There's shampoo on the shelf and a hair dryer under the sink, if you want it. Can you think of anything else you need?"

I need my mother, I wanted to say, but the words stuck in my throat.

"Livvy?" said Jessie Barnes.

"I need to know about you and Althea, and were you best friends, and if you were how come I never *heard* of you. I need to know if you always knew you were going to get me—if something happened to her, I mean."

She came and sat across from me, brushing the crumbs on the table into a neat little pile before she spoke. "Your mother and I weren't *best* friends, Livvy, but in an odd opposites-attract kind of way, we were *good* friends. We roomed together for most of our first year in college, and during that time we did our best to change each other: she tried to teach me to have more fun, and I tried to teach her to get her papers in on time. After Althea left, we kept in touch only intermittently—a note here or there, a postcard, a Christmas card, though I do remember that when you were born she sent a picture."

"Is that when she told you—about getting me?"

The refrigerator hummed and a truck went down the alley. "I'm not going to lie to you," Jessie Barnes said after a while. "I didn't know—not until Fred called the week after your mother died."

There was another long, stretched-out time while I stared at the pile of crumbs on the table and wanted to scatter them every which way.

"I didn't know, but I wasn't surprised," she went on, "because the two things I remember best about your mother were that she was never predictable—and that she had the habit of giving the most wonderful gifts. I can only say that now she has given me her most wonderful gift. Okay?"

She brushed the crumbs into the palm of her other hand and got up to empty them into the sink. Why'd you say yes—when Fred called? I had the words all ready, on the tip of my tongue, but before I could push them out, Jessie said, "I have something for you. Wait a minute."

I heard her go to her room, and in a minute she was back, reaching for my hand and putting something inside it. I looked down at a chunk of yellow polished glass on a shiny black cord, holding it up after a moment and watching it swing back and forth.

"Althea gave this to me the day she left college. For a couple of days before, I'd been struggling over a poem for English Lit that began 'Go, and catch a falling star,' and she told me this was my own private piece of a fallen star. I knew it wasn't, of course. I knew it was only glass, but still—well, you know that with your mother anything was possible. It's what *my* mother would call a lavaliere. And it's yours now."

I put the cord over my neck and let the star part hang outside my nightshirt. Then I got up and went down the hall to my room, closing the door behind me. I leaned against the inside of the door, thinking that I'd asked Jessie Barnes a question and she had answered me. And that as answers go, it was okay.

But I still don't want to be her kid. You hear that, Althea? I still don't want to be her kid.

4

Guess what, Althea! I have a cat. I got him at The Turnabout Shop, only he wasn't a regular turnabout like a chair or a bowl or a candlestick. But in another way I guess he was, because he used to belong to someone else and now he belongs to me.

I should probably back up and tell it the way it happened, though.

First we went to the shop, which is on a street with a couple of other stores and a lot of houses that are old and pinched-looking and have doors opening right onto the sidewalk. Without any porches or steps, I mean. Sitting on the pavement in front of the window that has *The Turnabout Shop* painted across it in curly black-and-gold letters were two rocking chairs and a bookcase with a glass front.

"What keeps them from getting stolen?" I asked.

"My mother's eagle eye, I guess," Jessie Barnes said. "That and a little luck. The only thing we've ever lost was a truly hideous umbrella stand."

Jessie pushed the door open, and a bell jangled overhead just as the woman behind the counter called out "Livvy!" in a way that sounded as if she'd been waiting for me. She got up and ran toward us, her arms outstretched, and even though she was small and wiry, before I knew it, I was swallowed up in this enormous bear hug.

"You don't mind if I hug you, do you?" she said, letting me go and stepping back. "My daughter here's not much of a hugger, which is okay, too." She turned and smiled at Jessie before going on. "But I just had to hug someone I've been so excited about meeting. How was your trip? Were you exhausted when you got in? What do you think of Baltimore, though truth to tell, I guess you haven't had time to look around, have you? We all wanted to come down to the station—Jessie's dad, Barney, her two sisters and her brother, the in-laws and all the kids. We even wanted to bring a banner with WEL-COME LIVVY emblazoned across it, but Jessie said we'd better wait. She thought it might all be a little over-whelming, and I guess she was right."

Jessie laughed and said, "You're doing a fine job of overwhelming her right now, Ivy." Then she gestured from her mother to me, from me to her mother. "Ivy, meet Livvy. Livvy, meet Ivy."

"We've met," Ivy and I said at the same time.

After that I wandered through the shop, running my fingers along tabletops, chair rungs, a pitcher made of squiggly glass. I breathed in the musty, waxy smell around me and wondered what it was about this place that made Jessie Barnes seem different—sort of like a hum waiting to be hummed. I half listened as she and Ivy talked about a pie safe that had been sold, thinking all the while about the furniture in our New York apart-ment and wondering what had become of it. Suddenly I had one of those swooping-down memories, Althea. It was of the day we carried that director's chair between us for seventeen blocks up Third Avenue while you chanted, "Flea market, flea market, we bought us a chair. We'll carry it home, and soon we'll be there."

"That's Depression glass, the pink," Ivy said, coming to stand beside me. And I blinked at the dishes lined along the top of the bookcase. "Oh," I said. "I wasn't ex-actly looking at that. I was thinking about our apartment in New York and wondering what happened to all the things—you know, the furniture and stuff."

"Fred's taking care of it," Jessie said. "But if there are things you especially want, I can call him and have him ship them when he sends the rest of your clothes and books."

I shook my head, staring hard at a platter that looked like a lettuce leaf and knowing, sure as anything, that I wanted to remember our old apartment just the way it used to be. That I wanted to be able to go from room to room in my head without any of the pieces missing.

Ivy nodded, as if what I hadn't said made perfect sense. "You know, I never met your mother, Livvy, but I heard a lot about her, back when the girls were in college, and I feel as if I knew her. You must miss her most dreadfully."

The words hung there, plain as day, for anyone to hear. *Miss her most dreadfully.* And I do—miss you most dreadfully, Althea. Most horribly and excruciatingly dreadfully.

"Yeah," I said as I turned away, my eyes sort of blurry, and stared at a ball of fur on a piano stool. All of a sudden, the ball moved and stretched and raised its head.

"It's a cat," I said, kneeling down on the floor and holding out my finger, watching as the cat curled one of his paws around it.

"Indeed, it is a cat," said Ivy, dropping onto the floor next to me. "He turned up in the alley behind the shop several weeks ago, just hanging out. I put an ad in the paper and flyers on a lot of lampposts in the area, but nobody's claimed him."

"What's his name?" I asked.

"Well, I've been calling him Mr. Max, but I'm not sure that's exactly right. What do you think?"

"How about just Max," I said, picking up the cat and feeling the way his paws sort of worked against my shoulder.

"Max, Max," said Ivy. "Yes, I think you're right, Livvy. Max *is* a better name, younger, with the ring of a *bon vivant*. When I took him to the vet's to have him checked out and get some shots, the doctor said he was actually just past kittenhood—more like a teenager, really."

"Does he live here?" I wanted to know.

"Well, he does and he doesn't," Ivy said. "I mean, he's *staying* here and seems reasonably satisfied, though I can't help thinking that late at night, when he's here alone and the walls are creaking and there's scarcely a car going by outside, he probably sits there on that piano stool and dreams of other living arrangements. Maybe someplace not quite so cluttered, someplace with windowsills and sofa cushions. Someplace that has people to have breakfast with, and dinner, too. You see, we're only here at the shop during the day, and not at all on Sundays."

"You could take him to your house," I said.

"Well, I thought of that," said Ivy, "but we already have three cats and a dog who's getting set in her ways. And I made a deal with Cider—she's the dog—that I wouldn't bring home any more cats, at least not unless I talked it over with her first. And every time I try to bring up the subject of Max to Cider, she dozes off or else goes into another room. That's the way dogs are, you know, hearing only what they want to hear."

Max wiggled out of my arms and went back to his spot on the piano stool, washing first one paw and then the other, and listening—I was pretty sure—to what we were saying.

"I *would* like to find a home for him," Ivy said.

"We could take him." The words popped out of my mouth before I knew they were coming. My face burned and I stared down at the floor.

"We *cou-ld,*" Jessie Barnes said, pulling at the word like a rubber band. "Yes, we could."

"What a wonderful idea," Ivy sort of sang out. "What a positively wonderful idea."

"It is a good idea," said Jessie Barnes. Then she laughed a laugh that was bigger than she was. "But tell me, Mom, why do I think this is what you had in mind all along?"

"Who, me?" said Ivy, reaching down to rub Max behind the ears. "Come on down to the basement with me, Livvy, and we'll find the cat carrier so you can take him right with you. I have extra food, too, though you and Jessie'll have to get your own litter box, because I need to keep one here for when one of my at-home cats comes for a visit."

I followed Ivy through the shop and down the stairs to the cellar, which was warm and dusty and filled with stuff. While Ivy rummaged for the cat carrier, I looked around at the clutter of boxes and chairs and a funky statue of a woman holding a lamp in one hand. "What's that?" I said, pointing to this huge wooden thing with strings going end to end.

"Oh, that's Jessie's loom. She's storing it here and hopes to get to work on it when things are slow upstairs—though the light isn't all that it should be. Here, I've found the box. Let's go."

Back upstairs, Ivy picked up Max, nuzzling her face against his before easing him into the carrier. "See, Max," she whispered, "I told you it would all work out. You take care now, and I'll come to see you soon."

Just then the phone rang. The bell over the door jangled as two women came in and stopped to look at a bulgy gold mirror with an eagle on top. "Come on,

Livvy," Jessie called, picking up Max's box and handing it to me. "This is my day off, and if we hang around anymore my mother will put me to work." She waved to Ivy and said, "We're off to the store."

"Good, good," Ivy said, walking us to the door. "I'll see you tomorrow, Jess, and, Livvy, you come anytime after school and just hang out. That's what my other grandchildren do."

Other grandchildren, other grandchildren. The words tickled inside my head as I followed Jessie to the car. Do you remember when I was really little, Althea, and asked you why I didn't have grandparents like other kids did. And how you told me about your parents being killed in a car accident when you were in college and how you dropped out afterward and headed west. And how we both sat there feeling sad until you grabbed a marker and drew smiley faces on us both and said, "I'm it, kiddo—mother, father, grandmother, grandfather, aunt and uncle."

And you were.

But anyway, to finish up the cat story: On the way home we stopped at the store, and Jessie ran in while I stayed in the car with Max, wiggling my fingers through the holes in the carrier for him to play with, wishing the whole time that it was you in the store, Althea. You who would come out carrying cat chow and litter and a litter box, Reese's peanut-butter cups as a special treat for us, and our favorite kind of blueberry yogurt.

You and not Jessie Barnes at all.

5

Anyway, Althea, I could tell from the start that it was going to be pretty cool having a cat. Particularly a listening cat like Max. The first thing I did when we got home, once I took him to my room, was tell him about you and show him the snapshot of the two of us the time we went to Ellis Island, and the falling-star lavaliere. Meanwhile, the nerdy girl and the fat rabbit were sort of giving him the evil eye. Max must have sensed it, too, because the hair on his back bristled and he settled on the foot of my bed with his paws tucked under and stared back at the picture. If you ask me, Max won the stare-off, because in a few minutes he turned away, stretching and batting at my fingers.

Next I showed him the litter box Jessie and I had set

up in the bathroom. Then she came in and told him to be sure to use it, and me to be sure to keep it clean and not let it get all gross and smelly. After that we ate lunch and Max checked out the apartment, including the corners and the backs of closets and even the top of the bookcase in the living room.

He must have worn himself out, because later in the afternoon, when Jessie had gone to the post office, he curled up under the kitchen table and fell asleep. I went out onto the fire escape, settling into a splotch of sunlight, looking back through the door at Max and watching, without being obvious about it, a girl on the fire escape two houses over who was watching me.

"Hey," she called after a while. "What are you doing there?"

"Looking at my cat. I just got him."

"No, I mean *there*, on that fire escape."

"I live here," I said.

"Since when?"

"Since last night."

"What happened to Jessie Barnes—the lady with the pulled-back hair?" she asked.

"She lives here, too. I live with her."

"You her long lost kid or something?"

"Or something."

"What d'you mean?"

"Well, I'm not her kid so I must be an 'or something,' right?"

"I reckon," the girl said. She stood up and leaned over the rail toward me. "Want me to come over?"

"If you'd like," I said.

"I'd like, but I'd better not, on account of my pop never wants me to go places where he doesn't know the people."

"Yeah," I said. "Althea was the same way."

"Who's Althea?"

"My mother."

"Oh. Did she leave and go to Chicago and have a bunch more babies like mine did?" the girl asked.

"Did who?"

"Your mom."

"No," I said.

"Oh, well, I'm glad. That she didn't move to Chicago and have a bunch more babies, I mean. My pop says it's rude to ask as many questions as I sometimes ask. Do you think it is?"

"Well, maybe. A little."

"Yeah. I've got to work on that. Anyway, why don't you meet me out front, and when Pop comes home I can introduce you and then he'll know you and I can come to your apartment sometimes if you want me to. Or you to mine. And I can tell you about Celery and Nadine and Charlie and even Robert."

"Who're they?" I asked, but before the words were halfway out, she had disappeared inside and slammed the door behind her.

A second later she was back, leaning over the railing and calling, "I'm Lu, with a *u* and not any *o*. Who are you?"

"I'm Livvy," I said, getting up. "And who're Celery and Nadine and—" But she was gone again, and I went inside and through the apartment and down the stairs and out the front door, where Lu was already waiting for me.

"Let's stay here, because your steps are better than my steps. More interesting and all," said Lu, sitting down and patting the spot next to her. "Did she tell you about the neighborhood? Did she tell you about me?"

"Did who?"

"Jessie Barnes. Didn't she tell you about me? How there was this girl about your age living two doors down who desperately needed *someone* to move in *somewhere*. How she—"

I shook my head and said, "I just got here from New York last night and then this morning we went to her shop and then we got Max and stopped at the store and then she talked about school and how I have to start to-morrow."

"Which school?"

I waved my arm and pointed in what I hoped was the right direction. "It's down that way and over some. Jessie took me past it on the way back this morning."

"Buckley Elementary," Lu said. "That's where I go. What grade?"

"Fifth."

"Me too, and I'll bet you'll be in my section, on ac-count of the other class has three more than ours. That means you'll have Ms. Crivello, who's really nice, even though in the beginning of the year I thought she looked a little like Cruella de Vil. You know, in the Dalmatian movie. Pop takes me in the mornings, and you can ride with us if you want, and then we can walk home to-gether. I'm a latchkey kid."

"Me too, I guess," I said, reaching into my pocket to finger the apartment key that Jessie had given me. And the weird thing was, Althea, that the thought of being a latchkey kid here in Baltimore made me feel tons lone-lier than it ever had in New York, where I never minded waiting for you to get home. To change the subject I asked, "Are they in Ms. Crivello's class, too—Celery and Nadine and Charlie and Robert?"

"Are they all in Ms. Crivello's class?" Lu sort of

choked, and I could tell she really wanted to laugh but was trying not to. "They're not kids. They're *grown-ups*, and all from this building."

"So what about them?" I asked, wiggling around on the top step and feeling the cold of the stone through my jeans.

"I'll get to that," said Lu. "And to telling you about the whole neighborhood and how the people in your building are more interesting than the people in my building, who are totally boring, except for Pop and me, and who leave every morning carrying attaché cases and come back every evening carrying attaché cases and take-out food. But first, what happened to her?"

"To who?"

"To your mom?"

"She died," I said. And you know something, Althea? I think that was the first time I ever said it straight out like that, to somebody who didn't already know, I mean. And you know something else? Part of me wanted to go on and tell Lu how sometimes it seemed that you'd been gone for ages and how sometimes it seemed that I was losing you for the first time all over again. "She died" was all I said, though.

"I'm really sorry," Lu said, and for a while after that neither of us said anything but just sat watching as a woman walked a three-legged bulldog down the other side of the street. "And I guess Pop'd say I shouldn't have asked, except if we're going to be friends, then we have to know that kind of thing. Don't you think?"

"Yes," I said, still with that sad, prickly feeling that thinking about you gives me, Althea. "But now tell me the stuff about the neighborhood and Robert and the rest."

"Okay," said Lu, taking a deep breath and sticking her legs out in front and sort of making circles with her feet. "First, the neighborhood, which is pretty cool except that there aren't enough kids our age 'cause it's filled with students and professors and old people and young couples with babies in strollers and bunches of dog walkers and you have to watch where you walk or else what you step in could be really gross. There's a deli on the next street over, where we sometimes go for Sunday breakfast, and a bagel shop and a video store with a lot of funky old black-and-white movies, including *Little Women* with Katharine Hepburn as Jo. And a block over from that is the park, only Pop won't let me go there by myself, or to the library, which is a string of blocks off in the other direction. On St. Paul Street is the bus to downtown and on Charles Street is the bus to uptown. And maybe someday we can ride the downtown bus all the way to the harbor. What d'you think?"

My head was spinning just from listening to Lu, and before I could answer, she went on.

"And now about this house—your house. In the basement are Miss Winston and her cat, Dudley, who looks like a bran muffin—Miss Winston, not Dudley—and is really nice and who sometimes has me run errands for her and gives me money as a tip, except Pop says I shouldn't take it because she's a neighbor. Then on the first floor are Nadine, a nurse, and Charlie, who is dashing and is always going places on his bike or roller blades. Then on the second floor are you and Jessie Barnes—"

"And Max the cat," I stuck in quickly.

"And Max the cat. And then on the third floor is Celery Stalk."

"Celery Stalk? Is that her name?" I asked.

"I'm sure it is," said Lu, nodding. "It says *C. Stalk* on her mailbox, but I can tell from the way she's skinny as a rail and is always jogging that her name really *is* Celery. She's a graduate student."

"How do you know all this?" I asked, thinking how I hardly knew anybody in our apartment building in New York.

"Oh, I just watch and listen a lot."

"And how about Robert?" I prodded.

Lu sighed and rolled her eyes. "Robert's, well, I secretly think he might be a movie star going incognito or a prince in disguise. He calls me Miss Lu, or Madame Lucrece, or sometimes 'girlfriend,' although I'm not, of course."

"Does he live here, too?"

"Uh-uh," said Lu, shaking her head. "But he's the manager of the apartments and collects the rents and sees to things. He's who you call when the heat's not working or when there's a problem with the plumbing. And I think maybe I'm going to be in love with him when I grow up. If I decide to be in love with anybody."

We sat there for a few more minutes and watched the traffic as it headed uptown. The air was suddenly cooler, and I rubbed my arms and said, "I'd better go."

"Don't leave yet," Lu said, looking at her watch. "Because any minute now my pop'll come around that corner from where he parks in back and you can meet him."

The words were scarcely out of her mouth when a man appeared, waving and calling to her. He was dressed in jeans and a windbreaker, with a backpack slung over one arm. He looked as if he was wearing Lu's face—the same wide mouth, the same squinchy lines around the

45

eyes when he smiled, the same curly dark hair. "Hi, girls," he said, coming up to us and dropping his backpack on the bottom step.

"Hi, Pop," said Lu. "This is Livvy. She's new here and lives with Jessie Barnes, the lady with the pulled-back hair, on account of her mother died and she's—"

"Slow down, magpie," Lu's father said, holding his hand out to me and saying, "Hi, I'm Ken Johnson and I'm glad to meet you."

"Ann Olivia Lyons," I said, standing up and taking his hand.

"Well, Ann Olivia, welcome to the neighborhood."

"She's Livvy, Pop," said Lu, sliding off the step to stand beside me. "And it's not just the neighborhood but the whole city. She came from New York last night, and tomorrow she starts at Buckley Elementary, and I said she could ride with us in the mornings if she wants and then we could walk home afternoons together."

"That'd be great," Mr. Johnson said. "Except that probably for the first few days Livvy's family will want to take her."

"She's not my family," I said. "She's not my anything."

Lu stepped back and for a minute no one said a word.

"Well, anytime you'd like a ride, we'd be happy to have you," Mr. Johnson said finally. He picked up his backpack and put his arm around Lu's shoulder.

"Yeah, see you," said Lu. Together they turned and started up the street to their building.

"She's Jessie Barnes is all," I called after them, but my words were swallowed by the rumble of traffic.

When I got back to the apartment, Jessie was sitting at the kitchen table with a man who had curly white hair and dark-rimmed glasses and was balancing Max on his knee.

"Hi, Livvy, I'm Barney," he said, putting the cat on the windowsill as he stood up—and up—and up. He was awesomely tall.

"This is my dad, Henry Barnes," said Jessie Barnes. "Only everybody calls him Barney."

"And I hope you will, too," Barney said, rooting in his briefcase for two brown paper bags and handing them to me. "These just called to me while I was out and about today. Go ahead, open them."

I opened one and peered inside, then looked up at him, not saying anything.

"It's okay," he said.

I shook the bag onto the palm of one hand and stared down at a small soft gray mouse. I looked at Barney, at Jessie, at Barney again.

"For Max!" I said all of a sudden.

"Catnip," he said.

47

"Thank you. But how did you—I mean, I just—"

"Oh, the jungle drums beat fast and furiously in this family," he said, laughing. "Besides, I was talking to Ivy a while ago. Now for the other one."

I reached inside the next bag and pulled out a skinny paperback book called *Millions of Cats*. Remember, Althea? It's the "millions and billions and trillions of cats" book we used to read when I was really little.

"Oh, thank you," I said, rubbing my fingers over the cover. "I love this book."

"Me too. It's my all-time favorite cat book, and even though it may be a little young for both of us, the way I look at it is that if it's the right book for the right person, then that takes precedence over age. Don't you agree?"

"I definitely do," I said, and when Barney held out his hand, we shook on it.

"Okay then, that done, I've got to be off," he said, turning to Jessie Barnes and giving her a quick hug. "You all take care, and welcome, Livvy. A royal welcome." And that quick, he picked up his briefcase and went out the back door, stopping only to rub Max behind one ear.

"Your father's nice," I said when I couldn't hear his footsteps anymore.

"Yes, he is," said Jessie Barnes, taking lettuce out of the refrigerator and starting to wash it.

"Your mother's really nice, too."

"I know. I'm very lucky. And by the way, I went ahead and fed the cat."

And then we hit another one of those walls of silence, as if we'd used up our talking allotment for the day. I wanted to hear about Barney. Wanted to tell her about meeting Lu and how maybe we were going to be in the same class, but once again the words stuck somewhere in my throat.

Besides, *she* didn't ask *me* where I'd been or what I'd been doing. What do you think of that, Althea? What do you think of your great Jessie Barnes now?

I mean, you could've put me with somebody who *talked.*

Couldn't you?

6

Jessie Barnes doesn't know *anything*, Althea. I mean, she has those books on her bedside table and a bunch more bookmarks at a bunch more pages, and she still thought I should wear a dress to school.

A *dress*? To *school*?

And you know what else? I'll bet there are tons more things to do with raising a kid that Jessie Barnes doesn't know, like how staying up late is good for a kid's health, and Snickers and M&M's are part of a well-balanced diet. And how tattoos are cool, and the "R" in R-rated movies really stands for remarkable.

I can't hear you, Althea. I've got my hands over my ears, so I can't hear you. Anyway, you're acting shocked and all just because you think you should. Because you're the grown-up. Besides, you wouldn't want me turning into a little khaki clone, would you? A junior Jessie Barnes.

Trust me.

For my first day at Buckley Elementary, I ended up wearing jeans shorts and my sunflower T-shirt with my falling-star lavaliere inside. Jessie took me and told Ms. Crivello (who, if you ask me, doesn't look that much like Cruella de Vil) about how I moved here from New York, but not the part about you, because I specially asked her not to. Mainly, I guess, because I didn't want anyone at *this* school to think my situation was Dickensian.

Ms. Crivello stood me up in front of the class and told everybody I had just come in from the Big Apple and now was their chance to find out everything they'd always wanted to know about New York. A boy with spiky black hair asked why they called it that, another boy asked how many miles of underground track were in the New York subway system, and a girl in a tremendous Orioles T-shirt wanted to know how the Yankees were going to do this season. I didn't know the answer to any of them, which was okay, because just at that moment the bell rang for a fire drill and we all tromped outside.

As soon as we got back in, we turned around and went out again, this time for recess, and by then everybody'd forgotten what they'd asked in the first place. The boys headed off to play ball, and Lu introduced me to Lawanda, Rosie, Maria, Katie, Toshiba, and a bunch of other girls. We mostly stood around staring at Lawanda, who had had her ears pierced the day before, and asking, "Did it hurt?" "Does it hurt now?" "What happens if you forget to turn the earrings and your ears get all gross and oozy?"

Buckley Elementary was newer than my school in New York and the ceilings weren't as high or the halls as echoey, but other than that, they seemed a lot alike: the same chalk and peanut-butter smell, the same kind of clock that scritched along, the same pizza in the cafeteria. I missed the kids in my old school, though, and in that sleepy after-lunch stretch of time I closed my eyes and pretended I was back there again, with Sally and Mary Claire and Monalisa and Jane. I came to in a hurry, though, when Ms. Crivello leaned down close to me and asked if I was okay.

Jessie was waiting for Lu and me after school and said that she and Ivy had worked it out so that she could leave the shop early in the afternoons for a while. "Until you feel at home," she said.

Hah! As if I ever would. Ever could.

"Well, how was it? How'd you make out?" she asked as soon as we were in the car.

"Okay, I guess," I said. And that was all I could think of to say. To Jessie Barnes, at least.

"It was fine. *She* was fine," said Lu. "In the beginning a bunch of kids asked Livvy about New York, but then we had a fire drill and she didn't get to tell them, and after that we just looked at Lawanda's ears on account of she had them pierced yesterday. I'm working on Pop to let me have my ears done. What about Livvy? You gonna let her have her ears pierced?"

Jessie rubbed one of her own unpierced earlobes and shook her head, sort of up and down and sideways, both at the same time, the way people do when they're not quite sure of things.

"Althea was," I said. "Going to let me, I mean. She promised to take me to have it done, only then she got sick and—and— You should've seen the tons of earrings my mother had, big ones that hung down to her shoulders and swung when she walked. Hoops and beads and dangly fish all in a row."

All of a sudden I was back in New York, on the day we went to the crafts fair where that friend of yours had a booth and we spent *hours* trying on necklaces and you finally bought the one that looked like pieces of cracked eggshells spattered with yolk. I was so far away that I didn't hear Lu getting out of the car. But then she called back over her shoulder, "I'll dump my books and phone

Pop and see you in a few minutes, if that's okay. Oh, and thanks for the ride."

We parked around back and went up the fire escape to the kitchen door, Jessie's questions clang-banging in the air the way our footsteps did on the metal stairs. "Did you like your teacher?" "Was the work hard?" "Did you make any friends?"

"I guess," I said as I went through the kitchen and along the hall to my room, closing the door and flopping onto the bed beside Max. I lay there for a while, rubbing the cat under the chin and thinking how it was all happening too soon. Jessie Barnes and this apartment and Lu, Ivy and The Turnabout Shop and Buckley Elementary. And even Max. How it was sucking me in. Like the time we went to the Jersey shore and the undertow caught me, and that cute lifeguard with zinc oxide on his nose had to save me. But who's going to save me now, Althea? Who?

I traced the words *I miss my mom* onto Max's back, the letters piling one on top of the other.

The doorbell rang from downstairs and a few minutes later I heard voices in the hall and after that a knock on my door. I quickly smoothed the cat's fur before Lu opened the door and came in, sitting on the foot of the bed and scooping Max up, dropping him onto her lap.

"Cool cat, cool room," she said, looking around.

Then, jerking her head in the direction of the door, she whispered, "She's got cupcakes out there, in the kitchen on a plate, just waiting for us to come eat them, I think."

"So let's go," I said, sighing, and as we opened the door and started down the hall, Max darted in front of us, his feet making little thumpy noises on the floor.

"I think she's nice," Lu said a while later when we'd settled ourselves onto the steps out front. "Jessie Barnes, I mean."

"Yeah, she is," I said. "She's really nice and she tries really hard and she has these really fat books to help turn her into a mother-person, but—but—"

"But she's not your mom," said Lu.

"Yeah, she's not."

"I know how you feel," Lu said. "After my mom up and went to Chicago—"

"No, you don't know how I feel. It's not the same thing at all," I said, my voice suddenly shrill. "Althea was a terrific mother and we used to do about a million things that were fun every week, and besides that, she didn't just *leave*. She *died*." I stopped for a minute, squashing back the times in the last few weeks when I'd felt angry at you for dying, Althea. For going off and leaving me alone.

"She used to dance," I said. "Around the apartment,

and once in Central Park, in the snow with the wind blowing every which way."

"My mom was terrific, too," Lu said, her voice small and flat and not at all the way it usually sounded. "At least I thought she was, until she left Pop and me and went off with somebody else."

I sat staring at the toes of my tennis shoes and wishing I could gobble back my words. "I'm sorry," I said after a while. "I'm really sorry."

"It's okay," said Lu. "And now I have Pop."

A couple of minutes later, the woman with the three-legged bulldog went down the other side of the street and waved to us and we waved back. "Come on," said Lu, "let's go somewhere."

"Go where?"

"Anywhere, everywhere, nowhere special," Lu answered. "Except that Pop says the city's not what it used to be. That when he was a kid, he and his sister both could go all over town, hopping on buses and off buses, or riding their bikes, exploring places on their own. Has Jessie Barnes given you the there're-a-lot-of-weirdos-out-there lecture yet?"

"No," I said.

"She will. Just you wait. But anyway, the deal I made with Pop is that I'm allowed to hang around out front, but if I want to go anyplace else, I have to go in and tell him, or call him if he's at work, and then when I'm back I have to tell him that, too. Which is sort of a pain, so sometimes I stretch the right-out-front part to include around-the-block. Come on."

But before we could even get up, there was a swooshing, rushing, roaring sound, and a figure dressed all in black swooped down in front of us, doing a slow turn and zigzagging backward.

"It's just Charlie on roller blades," whispered Lu as he swept the hat off his head, skimming it across the ground and bowing.

"Charlie Farley at your service."

"What're you doing here?" Lu asked.

"Waiting for Nadine, who's inside gathering clothes for the dry cleaners. Who's your friend?"

"This is Livvy and she's just moved in with Jessie Barnes on the second floor on account of her mother died and she's come from New York."

"Hey, that's rough," he said, turning to me and holding up one hand so that without thinking I slapped him five. "Really rough," he said. "Not the Jessie Barnes part, but—well—you know what I mean." He glided into a slow, loopy figure eight on the sidewalk in front of us and then came back, knocking on the first-floor window and waiting till a blond-haired woman holding a bunch of coats and sweaters opened it and leaned out.

"Nadine, meet Livvy," Charlie called. "She moved in on the second floor, so from now on if there's any rumpus and ruckus up there, just grab your broomstick and bang on the ceiling and tell her to cool it. Come on out."

He spun off in the direction of the door to the basement apartment, and in a minute he was back with someone I knew had to be Miss Winston, just from the way Lu had described her. I mean, she *did* look like a bran muffin.

"Oh, I love meeting new people," Miss Winston said, coming to sit beside me and taking my hand. "You'll stop in for tea one day soon, won't you? You be sure and bring her, Lu," she said, dropping my hand and reaching for Lu's. "I enjoy company, and so does Dudley—he's my cat, you know—and I like to bring in as many friends from the outside world as I can manage. Why, if I lived in the country, Dudley would run free from morning until night, but you can imagine what would happen if he got out around here, with all this traffic." She made a sudden splat noise with her hands, and for a minute we all sat there, trying *not* to imagine what would happen to Dudley.

"Oh look, here comes Celery," said Lu, pointing down the street.

"*Celie,*" said Charlie.

"*Celery*," said Lu. "I mean, her mailbox says C. Stalk and she looks like celery."

"She's got red hair," I said, studying the young woman coming toward us. "How can she look like a celery stalk if she has red hair?"

"You have to squint a little and think green," said Lu.

"Yeah," we all said, squinting and thinking green.

"You're right," said Nadine, who had come outside and was sitting on the top step. "The green sweats help, too, and the way her hair sort of flops and bounces, like the leafy top part of celery."

We watched as she got closer, her steps long and quick, her arms swinging by her side. "Hi, everybody," she said, stopping in front of us. "What's new?"

"Livvy is. She lives here now," Lu said, nodding in my direction.

"That's great," Celie said, holding out her hand to me. "I hope to see you around a lot, but right now I've got to run. I have a class and I need to get a shower before I go."

"We've got to be on our way, too," Nadine said, getting up and rearranging her bundle for the dry cleaners.

"And I have bran muffins in the oven I have to see to," Miss Winston said.

At first Lu and I tried not to look at each other, but then we couldn't not look any longer, and all of a sudden we were doubled over laughing. "Bran muffins, bran muffins," sputtered Lu, clapping her hand over her mouth. And you know something, Althea? That made me laugh even harder—a hold-your-stomach kind of laughing I never thought I'd do again.

When we caught our breath and looked up, everyone was gone, but in a minute Charlie came back, calling my name and beckoning to me. "Look, Livvy," he said. "If you ever need anybody to talk to, keep me in mind, okay? I've sort of been there, done that."

"What do you mean?" I asked.

"I know it's not the same, but when I was nine my mother got sick and my father couldn't manage so he sent me off to live with my aunt in Duluth for a while."

"Was it awful?"

"Oh, dreadful. She had mile-long fangs and spouted fire when she breathed."

"No, I mean it—was it *awful?*"

"Awful? No. Different? Yes," Charlie said. "But actually it was okay once I let go and gave it a chance. Anyway, kid, hang in there." And he was off, sailing along the street to catch up with Nadine.

That night, Jessie Barnes and I went to the deli around the corner for supper. We had chicken-salad sandwiches and I told her about meeting the people in the building and she said they were all good neighbors and I said, "Yeah," and that was about the end of it.

When we got home, Robert was standing on a ladder replacing a lightbulb in the downstairs hall. Jessie introduced me, and he saluted, first her, then me, and called down, "Great news, Ms. Barnes. Now you got yourself a kid."

"I'm not her kid," I hissed when I got even with his face as I followed Jessie up the stairs. "I'm not her anything."

And you know what else, Althea? If you want my honest opinion, Robert doesn't look like a movie star going incognito, or a prince in disguise either.

7

"The *whole day*? I've got to spend the whole day at The Turnabout Shop?"

"Well, yes, I'm afraid so," said Jessie Barnes, getting up and taking her breakfast dishes to the sink. "Would you like to call Lu and ask her to come with us?"

"She's going to the dentist," I said. "But the point is, it's Saturday and I—" *I what?* I suddenly asked myself. *I what? I what? I what?* "I've—got stuff to do."

"You can bring your schoolwork with you. There's a desk in the office in back that you can use."

Schoolwork? On Saturday? I wanted to scream. Do I look like somebody with nothing but schoolwork to do on Saturday?

"Ivy won't be coming in today because she wants to

get ready for the family dinner tomorrow, and Vernon, who works for us, has gone to Philadelphia for his niece's wedding." Jessie went on as if I weren't screaming in my head. As if she didn't hear me.

"Why don't you call Lu anyway and see if her father can drop her off after the dentist. Then run along and take your shower. We'll leave as soon as you're ready," she said in a that-settles-it voice.

Can you *believe*, Althea? I mean really, *can you*? I peeled off my clothes and turned on the water as hot as I could stand. Saturday, The Turnabout Shop, Jessie Barnes, and me. *Now, do something,* I thought, lathering my hair. *Do something, do something.* I closed my eyes and kept them closed as I stepped out of the tub, fumbling for my towel and drying myself all over, sure that when I opened them again you would have taken care of things. That I would be back in our old bathroom in New York with the missing tile over the sink and the pebbly glass in the tall, skinny window.

But when I did (open them), you hadn't and I wasn't. And Jessie Barnes was on the other side of the door, calling for me to hurry up.

The shop was dark and musty, and no Ivy waited to give me a hug, no Max sat on his piano stool. Jessie hurried around, turning on lights and the little radio in the far back corner, dragging the rocking chairs and the bookcase outside, and going on about estate sales and auctions and unexpected treasures. I couldn't believe it, but Jessie Barnes was suddenly a motor mouth.

I looked around for someplace to hide, for a hole to crawl into, but before I could find it, Jessie handed me a feather duster as if it were the Olympic torch or something, and set me to work. "Gently, gently," she called after me. "Just a flick of the wrist."

I wandered around, flicking my wrist at a weathervane in the shape of a grasshopper, a china-headed doll, a little box with writing on top that said *Love the Giver,* and a painted tin watering can. I picked up a cut-glass something that looked a lot like a baby rattle, but I was pretty sure wasn't, turning it this way and that.

"It's a knife rest," Jessie said, coming up behind me. "I found several of them at a sale down on the Eastern Shore, and you can't imagine how thrilled I was."

"Totally weird," I mumbled under my breath as I turned away, trailing my duster over a bunch of baskets and boxes and a cast-iron rabbit doorstop (actually *half* a rabbit, as if he'd been sliced down the middle), and setting all the crystals on this ancient glass lamp to jangling. Once I'd finished a quick tour of the shop, I sat down on Max's piano stool, spinning slowly one way and then the other. From there I moved to a prissy-looking straight chair, leaning back and closing my eyes, crossing my arms over my chest, and wishing I were someplace else.

I heard voices around me, but they sounded drifty and far away, and I didn't try to catch hold of what they were saying. A few minutes later, someone touched my shoulder, and when I opened my eyes, Jessie was leaning over me, with what looked like a mountain of cloth in her arms. "I need you to help me, Livvy. A customer's back for another look at one of the quilts. Come on over here and we'll hold it up for her."

I followed Jessie to the side of the shop where there was a sort of clear space and we opened the quilt, each of us holding on to a corner and letting it hang down between us while a woman with streaky gray-black hair stood watching.

"My, you're lucky to be able to help your mother in the shop like this," she said.

"She's not my mother." The words came quickly and filled the corners of the shop. I had dropped my end of the quilt and scrabbled around on the floor to pick it up again. "She's not my—"

"Oh no," Jessie said, "but Livvy's come to live with me. Her mother and I were roommates in college."

You see, Althea. It's going to keep happening like

that—people thinking I'm her kid. Maybe I should get a SHE'S NOT MY MOTHER sign. And wear it around my neck at all times.

"Well, you're a lucky young lady anyway, surrounded by all these pretty things," the witch-woman jabbered on, standing back to examine the quilt.

Jessie laughed. "Oh yes, maybe we'll make an antiques dealer out of her yet."

No way, I wanted to yell. No way is anybody turning me into some musty-dusty antiques person who gets her kicks out of moldy old stuff. I clutched my corner of the quilt, watching my fingers turn red and then white while I listened to Jessie and the woman.

"That's a tree-of-life design," said Jessie, pointing to something in the center. "See how it's all put together with triangles and how the greens and browns against the off-white background give it a rather serene look until you get to that splotch of yellow off to the side, which somehow manages to make the whole thing terribly vibrant."

I leaned forward, squinting at the shape Jessie had called a tree of life and wondering how she knew that—and what a tree of life was. And how she could get so totally worked up over it.

"I can't help thinking about the people who made this," the woman said, coming forward and taking my end of the quilt. "I mean, look at these stitches—and every bit done by hand."

"I'm like that about all the things I deal with in this business," said Jessie, helping her to fold the quilt. "It's as if each one has a story to tell. My mother and I always want to know who made them, who owned them along the way, what their lives were like. I guess in a small way we like to feel we're rescuing a part of the past from neglect."

"I'm going to do it—today," the woman said, digging her checkbook out of her purse. She and Jessie headed for the back of the shop and I wandered over to a table, flipping through a box of old postcards and reading messages written in ink that was faded and brown.

"She bought it?" I asked when the woman had left, her arms tight around a brown paper package.

"She bought it."

"Just like that?"

"Oh no," said Jessie. "She's been in here to look at it several times."

"And now she's going to take it home and put it on the bed and sleep under it and maybe spill coffee on it and have the dog jump on it and leave dog hair all over it?" I asked, remembering the thousands of tiny stitches, the tree of life, and the splotch of yellow in the far-down corner.

"Uh-uh," said Jessie, shaking her head. "She's going to hang it on a wall in her living room."

"On the wall?" I screeched, looking to see if she was kidding me. "A quilt on a wall?"

"People do that a lot, especially with these very old pieces. I've got a picture—I'll show you."

I followed Jessie over to the desk, took the book she held out to me, and stood looking at the picture even after she went off to help a customer.

Did you know that, Althea? That people hang quilts on walls? And if you did, how come you never told me?

Lunch was a non-occasion. Jessie sent me down to the corner store for tuna-fish sandwiches, and when I got back, we sat in the office part of The Turnabout Shop listening to each other crunch celery and not saying anything. After a while, the bell on the door jingled and Jessie went up front to talk to a woman who called out in a high fluty voice that she was looking for carpet balls. Whatever they were. I stayed where I was, slouching down in my chair and staring at a little card tacked up over the desk. "Things of quality have no fear of time," it said, and the word "time" seemed to pulse and blow up before my eyes.

"Time, time, time," I whispered as I slid lower in my

chair and thought of the afternoon stretching out ahead of me. Soon I got a crick in my neck and stood up, bunching my sandwich papers into the trash can, then headed back to my postcards. I thumbed through scenes of Atlantic City and Niagara Falls, turning each card over as I watched the words "Wish you were here" jump out at me.

Wish you were here. Wish you were here.

Wish you were here, Althea. Wish you were here.

"Hey, this is awesome," Lu said, coming up in back of me, picking up a kaleidoscope and holding it to the light. "This whole place is awesome." She put the kaleidoscope back on the table and reached for a fan, peering at me over the top. Then she was off, weaving in between chairs and tables and a chest of drawers with colored glass bottles lined along the top. She spun the spinning wheel in the corner and stopped in front of the bulgy gold mirror with the eagle on top, which made her look all wide-mouthed and pop-eyed, before circling back to where I was standing.

"Don't you think so?" said Lu.

"Think so what?"

"That it's awesome."

"I guess, a little," I said. Except it's old and dusty and

belongs to Jessie Barnes, I wanted to say, but before I could shape my mouth around the words, Jessie finished with a customer and came to join us.

"Are there any toys?" Lu asked. "You know, old-fashioned ones, the kind kids played with a long time ago."

"Yes," said Jessie. "There are a couple of dolls on that table over there and another whole bunch down in the basement that I've been meaning to put on display."

"Can we do it now? Livvy and I?"

"Sure, that's a great idea," Jessie said. And before I knew what had happened, she was clearing off a table in the front of the shop, and Lu and I were running back and forth to the cellar, bringing up dolls, a tea set, a Mickey Mouse dressed like a cowboy, a bank in the shape of a whale that swallowed pennies.

Lu picked up a curly-haired doll in a faded blue dress and sat her on the table, arranging the tea set in front of her. "What d'you think she'd say? What d'you think she'd have to tell us?"

"Who? What would *who* have to tell us?"

"The doll—this doll. And all the others, too. And Mickey Mouse and the whale, and that wooden dog over there. About where they've been and what they've been doing all these years."

"Dolls can't talk. Or toys either," I said, feeling mean

and grouchy and thinking maybe Lu was getting into this whole Turnabout Shop thing more than I really wanted her to. "Dolls just sit there." I flicked the one in the blue dress with my finger, half hoping she'd fall forward into her teacup.

"Don't be too sure," said Lu, arranging a set of alphabet blocks on the other end of the table. "I have this book from when I was little—well, actually it was Grammy's from when *she* was little, and she sent it to me when I was eight. Anyway, it's all about this doll named Hitty and the stuff that happened to her—a hundred years' worth. And she tells it."

I squinted at the doll on the table, trying to imagine her story, while Lu went on. "What d'you think *our* dolls would say about *us*—from when we were kids, I mean. I left my rag doll out in the rain one night when I was six, and she might still be blabbing that to anyone who'll listen. What was your favorite?"

"Kirsten," I said. "She's with my things that Fred the lawyer's sending from New York. Not that I *play* with her anymore, but still—"

"Yeah, I know," said Lu. "Molly's still on the bookcase in my room, except her hair's all frizzy because I used to take her braids out and then Pop and I together could never manage to get them right again."

"Yeah, I kept doing the same thing with Kirsten, but

Althea could always fix her up on account of she'd had a lot of practice with that one long braid down the middle of her back. Althea, I mean."

I closed my eyes and thought back to the Christmas when you gave Kirsten to me. Remember, Althea? It had been snowing that day and the three of us had gone out for a walk, you and I catching snowflakes on our tongues and Kirsten safe and dry under the umbrella between us.

At the end of the afternoon, Lu and I dragged the things in from the sidewalk out front and Jessie turned off the radio and the lights.

"Well, Livvy," she said, "I hope your day wasn't too boring."

"It was okay," I said.

"Think of something special you'd like to do next Saturday. Ivy will be in the shop, and so will Vernon."

"Get my ears pierced," I said, almost without thinking.

"We'll see," Jessie said, locking the door and heading for the car.

Okay, Althea—explain that one. How come if Jessie Barnes doesn't know anything about being a mother-person, she already knows to say "We'll see"?

8

What I want to know, Althea, is how can all these kids be my cousins when I'm not even related to Jessie Barnes or she to me? But all morning on the day of the big family dinner, she kept talking about the cousins this, the cousins that. And once, when she probably thought I wasn't listening, she snuck in a *your*. As in *"Your* cousins can't wait to meet you."

They're not my cousins.

And I can wait to meet them. Maybe forever.

Another thing, Althea. Except for Ivy, whom I really like, and Barney, who's cool and brought me the book and Max the mouse, how come all of a sudden I need these people—aunts and uncles and cousins and stuff. I mean, you and I always managed to get along fine without anybody else, when it was just the two of us. Didn't we?

"What if they don't like me?" I said, slouching down in the front seat of the car as Jessie backed out into the alley.

"Of course they'll like you."

"They might not."

"They will."

"How do you know?"

"I just do," she said, setting her mouth into an I'm-right-and-you're-wrong kind of a line.

What if they think I'm a nerd? A loser? I wanted to keep going, but didn't. What if they say, "Aunt Jessie, send her back," and you *do,* on account of you've known them longer than you've known me. What happens then? I mean, I certainly didn't want to be here, but suddenly the thought of those bossy cousins trying to get rid of me made me want to dig my toes in and hang on. The way I did at the beach when the waves washed backward out to sea.

"Let's run through it one more time," Jessie said, her voice yanking me back to the present. She started in again, the way she had the night before at supper, spinning out names and ages and which kid was whose. How she had two sisters, Meaghan and Susan, and a brother named Paul. And there were three cousins named Meg, Susie, and Paulie, except that Meg was Susan's kid, Susie was Paul's, and Paulie was Meaghan's. Then there were two other cousins, Noah and Nell, and Noah was Susie's brother, and Nell was Meg's sister. There were also two brothers-in-law and a sister-in-law ("We'll get to them later"). And of course there was Cider the dog and a bunch of cats.

I was still trying to get everyone straight when we pulled up in front of the house and I saw about a million people waiting on the porch. Right away I wanted to crawl down under the seat and never get out of the car.

Except I did. (Get out of the car.) Mostly on account of you, Althea, and the way I could sort of feel you pushing me from the inside out, could almost hear you whispering, "Shape up, kid," the way you used to when you thought I wasn't going to.

And because Ivy and Barney had come down off the porch and were standing on the sidewalk, waiting for me. But no sooner was I out of the car than this whole mob of kids appeared behind them, carrying a banner that said WELCOME, LIVVY, swarming around and capturing me, moving me farther up onto the lawn.

"Are you Livvy?" asked a little girl in a polka-dot dress.

" 'Cause if you are, then you're our cousin," said a girl with a ponytail.

"Well, I—I—" But before I could go on, a boy with red hair who had to be about my age broke in. "Ivy *said* so. She told us a bunch of times over."

"How you're *real*, the way Meg and Nell and Paulie are real cousins to Noah and me," said a girl with the same red hair.

"And we're supposed to make you welcome because you might feel strange and all."

"And you're going to live with Aunt Jessie."

"I thought new cousins were babies."

"Some are and some aren't. It's like with dogs, the way some are puppies and some come fully grown, like Cider from the SPCA."

I held my breath and crossed my fingers and hoped nobody'd ask me if I came from the SPCA. But before I really had to worry, the redheaded girl said, "I'm Susie and that's my brother Noah. And the one with the pony-tail is our cousin Meg."

"I'm their cousin and Nell's sister," said Meg, catching hold of the girl in the polka-dot dress and spinning her around. "And *he,*" she said, pointing to a little boy in a shark T-shirt, "is Paulie, and he's four and everybody's cousin and nobody's brother."

"Grrrrrrr," said Paulie, making a shark face and lunging at me.

I was just trying to get it straight, saying Noah and

Susie, red hair; Meg, ponytail; Nell, polka-dotted dress; Paulie, shark shirt, over and over to myself, when the rest of the grown-ups came swooping off the porch to join us.

"Hi, Livvy, and welcome," said a woman who looked sort of like Jessie, only taller, holding out her hand to me. "I'm Aunt Meaghan and this is my husband, Bill, my sister Susan, and my brother-in-law, Bob."

"And I'm Jessie's brother, Paul," a man spoke up. "And here's my wife, Gloria."

Names and faces and sights spun around me. I felt as if I were being sucked into a whirlpool. Ponytail—shark shirt—polka-dotted dress—Cider—WELCOME, LIVVY. Down, down, down, twirling, swirling. Smiles and hands reaching out to me.

One hand caught hold and pulled me away from the center. "Come on," said Noah, calling over his shoulder for Susie to follow us. "I'll show you where we go when we want to hide out."

A few minutes later, we had settled onto broken-down chairs around a broken-down picnic table in the far back corner of the yard behind the garage. "Ivy was going to get rid of this when they got the new stuff, but Barney told her not to," said Noah. "He told her that everybody needs a place to get away to—and this is ours. Besides, he repots his plants back here."

I stared down at the gouged-out tabletop, wondering

what I was supposed to say and wishing I'd stayed out front, where with all the commotion I wouldn't have had to open my mouth.

"Is it weird?" asked Noah, pushing his fingers through his hair. "Being here, I mean. With all of us."

Susie jabbed him with her elbow. "No-ah, don't *say* that."

"Why not? I can. Besides, I want to know and Livvy doesn't mind me asking. Do you?"

"Uh-uh," I said, shaking my head. "I don't mind you asking, and yeah, it *is* sort of weird."

"Because there're so many of us?"

"Because there're *any* of you." I picked up a lopsided pinecone and tried to spin it across the table.

"You mean us? The cousins?" said Susie.

"You. The cousins. And everybody else, too. Aunts, uncles, grandparents. Because before, it was just Althea and me," I said, picking up the pinecone and trying again.

"Althea was—"

"My mother."

"Who was Aunt Jessie's friend, right? Ivy told us. But who'd you do stuff with?" Noah said.

"Althea."

"Who else?"

"Althea, I *told* you."

78

Noah and Susie looked at me, at each other, and back at me again. "That might be interesting. And okay, I guess. But in this family we do a lot together, all of us," said Noah, pointing toward the house. "We go camping and—"

"But not Ivy and Barney," Susie broke in. "Not till they invent a tent with a tile bath attached, Ivy says."

"We have birthday parties and cookouts, and in the summer we usually go to the beach for a week and stay in two houses across the street from each other. Can you swim?" Noah asked.

"Not really," I said. "Althea and I went to the Jersey shore a couple of times, but we didn't exactly swim."

"You'd better learn, then," said Noah. "You'd better get Aunt Jessie to send you for swimming lessons. To the Y, where the rest of us went."

And before I could figure out how I was supposed to get Jessie Barnes to send me for swimming lessons, Susie was tugging at my arm and saying, "Come on, we'll show you around the house."

We started in the basement, which was cold and damp, with a giant pool table in the middle. From there we went to the first floor, trailing through the sun porch, where the grown-ups were watching a basketball game on TV, the living room, the hall, the dining room, and on to the kitchen, where Meg and Nell were playing

Chutes and Ladd₋ ₋ with Paulie. Then we ran up the back steps to the second floor.

"That's Ivy and Barney's room in there," said Susie. "And Aunt Meaghan and Aunt Susan were across the hall when they were little. Aunt Jessie was in the back, and our father was on the third floor, which is also where Ivy has her computer and a bunch of stuff to do with the shop. Come on, we'll show you."

"Where do you sleep?" said Noah, stopping at the foot of the stairs and looking at me.

"Where do I sleep where?"

"In Aunt Jessie's apartment," he said.

"In the guest room," I said.

"There isn't any guest room."

"Sure there is—'cause I'm in it. You know, the room with the spool bed and the picture of the girl with the fat white rabbit."

"There isn't any room with a spool bed and a fat white rabbit."

"There is, too, and I sleep in it."

"Where is it, then?" asked Noah.

"It's the one first thing off the living room as you head down the hall to the kitchen."

"*The loom room?* You sleep in the *loom room?*" Susie and Noah screeched together.

"The loom room?" I said. "What's a loom room?"

"A room for a loom—Aunt Jessie's loom. You know, for weaving and stuff, with enough space left over for a sleeping bag on the floor for when one of us slept over," Susie explained.

"Is it big?" I said. "The loom? And made of wood, with strings going end to end?"

"They're called the warp, and the ones that go across are the weft threads, and the thing that sort of leads them over and under is the shuttle," said Susie. "Why?"

"I saw it," I said. "The loom. It's in the basement of The Turnabout Shop."

"Aunt Jessie's loom is in the basement of The Turnabout Shop?" said Susie.

I couldn't answer, but just stood staring at Susie and Noah. They stared back at me. Somewhere deep in the house a door slammed and Cider barked. And down at the bottom of my stomach a squiggly pain started up. *This is when it happens,* I thought. *This is when Noah and Susie and all the rest shout out, "Send her back, Aunt Jessie. Send her back."*

The dog barked again. Someone turned up the television sound and quickly turned it down. Time stopped and, ages later, began once more.

Noah crinkled his brows and looked at me for another minute before he turned and led the way up to the third floor.

We went through Ivy's office, stopping only to look out the window at the garage roof and the yard down below.

"Our father slept in this other room when he lived here, and it's still got a bunch of his old stuff in it—his beer-can collection and the ship model he and Barney made one time," Susie said as we moved across the hall and she pushed the door open.

I followed them into the room, but instead of looking at the beer cans or the ship model or any of the other things from when their father was little, I thought about Jessie Barnes. "What does she *do* with the loom? Your Aunt Jessie."

"She weaves," said Susie. "Really neat things like place mats and scarves and wall hangings. She even made this rug," she said, pointing to the floor.

I stooped down, running my fingers along one edge of the blue-and-green rug, then quickly pulling away and standing up again.

"All I can say is, Aunt Jessie must've really wanted you to come," said Noah. "Because once I tried to talk her into turning that room in her apartment into a place where I could keep my snakes and she said, 'No way.' Come on, let's go down."

At the second-floor hall we stopped to look at the pictures lined along the wall. There were brides and babies and people in caps and gowns. There were kids in bathing suits and a boy holding a fish by its tail who I thought was Noah but turned out to be Paul when he was little. Jessie Barnes and Meaghan and Susan and Paul, from a long time ago, were on the corner of the porch, eating ice-cream cones—and Meg, Susie, Paulie, Noah, and Nell stood in the same corner, years later, also eating ice-cream cones.

I reached out and touched one of the pictures. "Jessie has this one on her dresser," I said.

"Yeah," said Noah. "It was taken at Barney's birthday a few years ago, and there we all are, even Paulie, only he's the baby Aunt Meaghan is holding."

"And who's that?" I asked, tapping the glass over the blond-haired man with his arm around Jessie.

"That was Hank," said Susie. "They were going to get married and I was supposed to be a flower girl and I already had a new yellow dress and was going to carry a basket with daisies inside."

"What happened?" I said.

"Aunt Jessie called it off," said Susie.

"She said Hank was a really great guy, but he wasn't 'right' for her," said Noah.

"And she and Ivy and Aunt Meaghan and Aunt Susan called up all the guests and told them not to come and sent the presents back, and my yellow dress, too."

"Hank *was* great, though. He did magic and pulled quarters out of our ears and knew about a zillion card tricks," said Noah.

"And on the day that was supposed to be her wedding day, we all went to a ball game, except for Aunt Jessie, who went to the movies by herself. And my mother said she bets she cried buckets."

For a minute, sort of in spite of myself, I felt really sad for Jessie Barnes, sitting in the movies and crying all by herself, even though *she* had called off the wedding and knew that Hank wasn't "right" for her.

And I felt sad for him, too.

When we got downstairs, it was almost time for dinner. The dining-room table had been stretched out so that it was about a mile long, and there were places set all around.

Everybody talked at once. Paulie hung on to my left leg, and Meg tried to push me into a chair between her and Susie. Aunt Meaghan poured milk, and Ivy and Gloria came in carrying pans of lasagna that they put at opposite ends of the table. Paul brought the salad, and Nell made it just to the edge of the rug before she dropped the Parmesan cheese. She stood and howled while Cider made a dive for the cheese, eating most of it before Barney got there with a dustpan and brush.

Noah grabbed the dog by his collar and shoved him to-ward the back door—"In case he barfs," he called over his shoulder. And Paulie let go of my leg and chased Nell around the table.

"Okay, everybody, grab a seat," Barney said.

All of a sudden I felt that I was caught in a gigantic game of musical chairs, except at the end of this game there was a place for everyone. For a minute, everyone kept quiet so that Ivy could say grace. But as soon as she'd finished, the noise erupted again.

Noah told Jessie Barnes I needed to take swimming lessons.

Aunt Gloria said maybe I'd like to go to art class with Susie once school was out.

Paulie sang the itsy-bitsy-spider song about a million times, until his mother told him to stop it.

The grown-ups talked about baseball and how the Orioles would do this summer.

Paulie sang about the itsy-bitsy spider again. This time under his breath.

What happened on the way home was totally weird for Jessie and me, because we kind of fell into a conversa-tion, the way regular people do, and kept on talking. For a while, anyway.

It started when I asked what I'd been wanting to ask

all along but hadn't had the nerve. "Why did you say yes when Fred called that day and asked would you take me? You could've said no."

"I could have, but I didn't. And I think I said yes for a bunch of reasons, but mostly because it seemed right to me," Jessie said.

"The way marrying Hank seemed wrong?" I asked.

"Not *wrong* exactly, but wrong for me, wrong for both of us," she said. "And I see that the cousins have been talking."

"Well, yes, a little. Because I asked about the man in the picture, and they told me about you sending the presents back and even Susie's flower-girl dress."

"Poor Susie. I think the whole thing was almost harder on her than on anybody else, though I thought for a while that my entire family, if they'd had a choice, would've kept Hank instead of me."

We stopped for a light, and when we started up again Jessie Barnes said, "Remember how I told you once that your mother gave the most wonderful presents? Well, I guess that's another reason why I said yes—because I knew you'd be really special. That and the fact that I have this terrific family, and though I knew that none of us could make up for what you'd lost, I figured they'd be a definite plus.

"And I remember one time, back in college, when I

was being super-cautious about something, Althea looked at me and said, 'I'm waiting for the day when you take a flying leap, Jessie Barnes. I'm just waiting for the day. And I hope I'm there to see it.' "

"And I'm your flying leap?" I asked.

"You're it," said Jessie Barnes. "And you know something, Livvy, I think, in a way, Althea *is* here to see it."

I nodded, and kept nodding, all the way home.

Later that night, I lay on my bed, petting Max and telling him about the cousins and the house and me maybe taking swimming lessons. I told him about Hank, too, and the wedding that wasn't and how we were sleeping in what used to be the loom room, and how I wondered whether Jessie wouldn't rather have her loom back instead of a kid (me) and a cat (him).

And I asked Max how he thought you knew, Althea. That Jessie Barnes would say yes, I mean.

9

"I'll give you a penny for them," a voice said, and I looked up to see Charlie squiggling backward to the curb on his roller blades.

"For what?" I asked.

"Your thoughts. A penny for your thoughts. Didn't anyone ever say that to you before?"

"Yeah, Althea did. And then when I'd tell them to her, she'd sometimes say that was a twenty-cent thought, or an eighty-cent one. And sometimes she'd just hand me a penny. But the ones I'm thinking now are sort of big and heavy and—"

"A penny's my best offer," said Charlie, gliding forward, then veering off to the left. "Unless, of course, you want me to sit down and listen to them."

"Okay," I said, scooting over to make room for him on the step.

"So," he said. "What's with these big and heavy thoughts?"

"Well," I said, stopping for a minute, then starting up again. "Well, it all has to do with yesterday, when we went to this family dinner at Ivy and Barney's—they're Jessie's parents—and about a million relatives were there, including these kids who are her nieces and nephews and now sort of my cousins."

"Were they okay? The kids, I mean."

"Yeah, they were nice, especially Noah and Susie, and kind of made me think cousins might be good to have. Except that almost right at the beginning, Noah asked me where I slept and I said the guest room and he and Susie said there wasn't one and I said there was and when I told them where it was, they screamed and said the loom room—you sleep in the loom room. And then I remembered how I'd seen a loom in the basement of The Turnabout Shop."

Charlie's face was blank and he stared at me. "So?"

"Don't you *get* it?" I asked.

"Afraid not. You'd better explain."

"It's like this. Jessie Barnes had a loom in her apartment, and now it's in the basement of the shop, where—"

"I know. Nadine and I helped her take it apart and put it on the truck she rented, and all the while Miss Winston was running up and down the sidewalk, wringing her hands, and Celie was calling instructions from the third-floor window," Charlie said.

"And now Jessie Barnes has a kid instead of a loom. That's what I've been *saying*—how it's on account of me—how it's all Althea's fault. And I told Althea last night that she should've thought of that, should've—"

"Who's Althea?" Charlie asked.

"My mother. I talk to her some. But promise me you won't say that to anyone. Okay?"

"Okay, but let me tell you something," he said, puffing his cheeks, then swooshing the air out of them. "Looms are looms—but kids are cool. Any more questions?"

"Well no, I guess not. If you're sure," I said, not totally convinced, but *wanting* to be.

"I'm positive," said Charlie. "My aunt in Duluth told me so."

"There *is* just one more thing, though," I said a few minutes later, when Charlie started to get up. "I mean, it might sound dumb, but Noah and Susie told me about a man named Hank who Jessie Barnes was supposed to marry only she called it off. Well, what happens if he comes back or she meets somebody else, like a prince or even a regular person, and gets married and maybe even has a baby?"

"She might," Charlie said, which wasn't what I wanted to hear at all. And I was pretty sure I felt the steps shake beneath me.

"What do you mean, she *might*?"

"She might. People *do*. And Jessie Barnes is really a great lady."

"But what'll we do then?"

"First thing, I figure, is get a new apartment, or maybe even a house with lots of room for you and the loom and the new baby," said Charlie.

"What baby?"

"The one you're convinced she's going to have when she marries the prince."

"I don't mean do about a house but do. You know, what'll we *do*?"

"Oh, *that* kind of 'do,' " said Charlie. "What you do then is move over some and make room, the way we always do when new people come into our lives.

"Same as we move the other way, filling in the spaces when someone goes out of our lives. But I suspect you know all about that by now."

I nodded, and for a while we sat on the steps, staring

at the traffic, until Charlie got up and slapped me five before taking off down the street and around the corner.

Special bulletin: Charlie's okay. And I'm going to hint to Jessie Barnes for roller blades for my next birthday if she asks, and if she even knows when my birthday is. Does she, Althea?

Lu arrived just before the UPS man, and we were sitting on the steps, talking, when the truck lumbered up and the driver got out, carrying a gigantic box wound all around with shiny brown see-through tape. "Packages for Lyons," he said. "Ann Olivia Lyons."

"That's me," I said, and before I knew it, he had gone back to the truck for another and another, until there were five in all, piled on the top step like a giant cardboard wall.

"Wow," said Lu, getting up to examine the boxes. "Is it your birthday or something?"

"No."

"Well, it's too late for Easter and too early for Christmas. Maybe you entered some fantastic contest and won the prize, *all* the prizes."

"I didn't."

"Maybe you—"

"It's my stuff," I mumbled, trying to swallow back the words.

"What stuff?" asked Lu.

"You know, I told you. My stuff from New York that Fred the lawyer sent."

"Your Kirsten doll, that you don't play with but's going to be an antique someday? And your books?"

"Yeah, that and my extra clothes, you know, for winter and all. Just stuff."

"Come on, then," said Lu, nudging a space open with her foot so we could get to the front door. "I'll help you take them upstairs."

We had thumped and bumped three boxes to the second floor when Robert came out of the basement and helped us with the other two. By that time, Jessie Barnes had opened the apartment door to see what the noise was all about.

"Let's put some of these in the living room so you'll have more room to unpack," she said.

But I was already shoving the largest box along the hall to my room. "No, I want them in here," I said, pushing and pulling until I'd crowded all five boxes between my bed and the window, trapping myself in the far corner. The girl in the rabbit picture seemed to scowl at me, and I looked away from her and turned to face Lu and Jessie, who were standing in the doorway. Waiting.

"Okay. Where shall we start?" said Lu. "You could unpack and hand us things and then we could put them places or pile them on the bed or—"

"I'll get scissors to cut the tape," Jessie said.

"No," I said, suddenly feeling prickly all over. "No. Not now. I mean, I'll get to them later." And I made my way across the room, forcing the two of them out into the hall and struggling to close the door behind us.

But later didn't happen. Not that night or the next day or even the next. The boxes sat there, and after a while I sort of got used to stepping around them to get to my dresser or closet, got used to piling my schoolbooks on one and watching Max sleep on another.

It was weird. Here were the boxes I'd been looking forward to getting, filled with everything I owned in the whole wide world, only now I didn't want to open them. *Couldn't* open them.

And I've been waiting for you to tell me what to do, Althea. Hear that? Waiting for you to take charge.

It was Jessie Barnes who finally did. On Friday we got out of school at noon because of teachers' meetings, and when I got home Jessie was at work and there was a note propped on the kitchen table.

Livvy— Please unpack your things this afternoon. *I found a bookcase at the shop that will be just right for your room, and I'll bring it home today. If you finish early and want to come over to the Turnabout, just call and Ivy or I will come get you. See you later. J.*

I left the note where I found it and ate lunch, chewing each bite of my sandwich for a really long time. I cleaned up the kitchen better than I ever had before, rubbing at a smudge of peanut butter on the counter long after it had disappeared and watering the plants on the windowsill, which were already soggy. I even carried my paper napkin and apple core all the way down the fire escape to the trash bin in the alley, rather than just tossing it in the can under the sink.

When there was nothing left to do, I grabbed the scissors and went along to my room, slitting the tops of the boxes one after the other and standing back to watch as they seemed to erupt, like a bunch of volcanoes, spilling everything I owned out into Jessie Barnes's guest room.

Sweaters, corduroys, turtlenecks tumbled to the floor. Snow boots and my winter coat fell on top of them. Books shot out of one of the boxes and I grabbed at them, piling them in the middle of my bed and running my fingers over the covers. *Madeline, Where the Wild Things Are, Mr. Popper's Penguins.* Remember, Althea, how we used to read them together, settled onto one end of the couch. *Harriet the Spy*, and *Caddie Woodlawn*, the *Little House* books. There was a surge of stuffed animals, and I caught my Kirsten doll up out of their midst, holding her close and smoothing her dress before I sat her on my dresser.

My Aslan poster was wedged catercorner across the bottom of the largest box, and I pulled it free, unrolling it and smoothing it flat against the closet door, fastening it with Scotch tape. I found my jewelry box in a tangle of mismatched socks and sat down on the floor to open it, to listen to the music and watch the ballerina dance. Remember how we used to do that, Althea, spinning and dancing round and round, holding on to each other when we could barely stand up. And how one time we made so much noise that Mr. Warner, in the apartment under ours, had to bang on the pipes to make us stop.

I reached for a small white box that had landed under a pile of T-shirts and pulled it out. A piece of paper was fastened around it with a rubber band, and I crawled up onto the bed before taking it off and reading what was there.

Dear Livvy,
Fred asked me to help pack your things—hope we haven't forgotten anything. And, oh, by the way, your pas-

tels are wrapped inside your winter coat. Just hope they didn't break! I also sent along some of your mom's earrings (little white box). I know they're too old for you now, but I thought you'd want to have them, as they're so typical of her. They are Althea.

Pete, the kids, and I think of you so often and hope things are going really well. Let us hear from you when you can, and remember, the sofa bed's ready and waiting anytime you want to come for a visit. Fred says he'll call next week to see if everything got there safely. Meanwhile—

Love from all of us,
Joannie

I opened the box and took the earrings out one at a time and held them up to my ears as I went to stand in front of the mirror, trying to imagine myself with pierced ears. But the dangling fish, the hoops, the beads and triangles just hung there, not swinging and swaying the way they did on you, Althea. Not swinging and swaying at all.

I crept back to my bed, sliding the box under my pillow and curling into a ball. And I cried. Big slobbery hiccuppy tears that got Max's fur wet when he came to lie beside me.

Some time later I rolled onto my back and Max climbed onto my stomach, staring at me with his yellow eyes and every once in a while giving me a nudge with one of his paws. I looked up at the ceiling, trying not to see all my New York things spilled out around me. But I knew they were there, same as I knew something else. That it wasn't pretend anymore. That you weren't just away on a trip. And that I wasn't going to get to go home.

I don't know how long I stayed that way, don't know whether I slept or not, but suddenly I heard the click of Jessie's key in the lock. I flew out of bed, grabbing handfuls of clothes and shoving them into the closet, the chest of drawers, and pushing the empty boxes into the hall.

"It's a big job, isn't it, Livvy?" said Jessie from the doorway. "It's a hard job." And she reached out with the tips of her fingers and touched me on the cheek. "Anyway, the bookcase is in the car, and whenever you're ready we can bring it in."

10

And that's why I haven't talked to you for a while, Althea. Because I've been feeling really mad at you—for leaving and not ever coming back. The weird thing is, though, that I miss telling you what's been going on in my life (nothing much).

It's too late now to catch up, so I'll just go on from here except to say that I didn't get my ears pierced on the Saturday I was supposed to because early that morning Lu called and said she and her father were off to Ocean City for the day and did I want to come along. That even though it was still too cold for swimming, we could hang out on the beach and the boardwalk and maybe go on some of the rides and eat French fries with vinegar and stop at the crab house for supper on the way home.

When I asked Jessie what she thought, she said it was up to me, but it sounded like fun and there'd be lots of Saturdays to get my ears pierced, and if I wanted to go, then why didn't I. So I did.

But there weren't lots of Saturdays to get my ears pierced. I mean, the next week Jessie had to work, and after that was the May festival at Buckley Elementary, which took up a lot of the day, and then there was work again, and one Saturday Jessie took Noah and Susie and me to the country to look at a bunch of antiques that turned out not to be antiques at all, but we had a good time anyway. Then work and a Saturday band concert, work and— This took us all the way up to when school let out and I started my swimming lessons and an art class with Susie, and hung out at The Turnabout Shop and around the neighborhood when Lu was there and not at her aunt's, which is where she has to go most summer days because the city isn't what it used to be and her father worries about her being home alone.

And okay, I know there were other times, like Sundays and nights and late in the afternoon after work, but somehow the great ear-piercing event never happened. Mostly, I think, because Jessie Barnes must have found something in one of her how-to-be-a-mother-person books that told her ways to keep from doing what she didn't want to do in the first place. Same as you used to,

Althea. Same as you used to. Like with the black down-to-my-knees T-shirt you almost didn't let me get—and the butterfly tattoo you definitely didn't let me get.

"You promised I could get my ears pierced and I never did," I said one Friday night when we had finished supper and were walking over to the video store for a movie. "And now I have the most boring ears in all the world." Except for you, I added to myself.

"I don't think I actually promised," Jessie said.

"You said 'We'll see,' and whenever somebody says 'We'll see' and doesn't say no right afterward, it pretty much means they're going to do it. At least, with Althea it did."

Jessie laughed. "I guess you're right. So, okay—if you're sure."

"I'm sure."

"Then how about tomorrow? My sister Susan told me about a place at the mall in Towson, the Earring Boutique, or something like that. We can go to lunch and then get your ears done. Maybe even look for some new shorts while we're out there."

My stomach did a sudden flip-flop, and I reached up to catch hold of my earlobes. "Maybe ears and *then* lunch," I said.

"Okay, whichever. But you know, Livvy, you don't

have to have this done. I think you look fine the way you are. Your ears are—"

"Dullsville. Bor-ing. Besides, I *do* want it. Haven't I been saying that like maybe forever?"

The next morning after breakfast, while Jessie was having one of her endless phone conversations with Aunt Meaghan, I went into my room and closed the door. I reached into the bottom of my underwear drawer and pulled out the box of your earrings, Althea, spilling them onto my bed and trying to decide which pair I liked best. "What d'you think?" I asked Max, who had come to sit beside me and was watching carefully as I circled my finger over them all, trying to choose.

"How about the fish?" I picked up the sort of silvery, dangling, big and little and in-between size fish and held them to the light.

"Yes, it should definitely be the fish," I said as I wrapped them in a Kleenex and shoved them down into my pocket.

It was late morning when we finally left the apartment, but it wasn't until we were pulling into the parking garage at the mall that I got my positively brilliant idea. "Why don't you get your ears pierced, too?"

Jessie Barnes stopped the car right on Level 4, not

even in a parking place, with cars lined up in back of her and one creep blowing his horn. "Who, me?"

"You could," I said. "You should. I mean, naked ears are so—"

"Bor-ing?" she said. "Dullsville?"

"Well, yes. Anyway, how come you never had them done, when you were young and all?"

"Well," she said, sounding a lot like a porcupine about to shoot its quills, "I like to think I'm *still* young and all, but if you mean why didn't I have my ears pierced back when I was in school and my sisters and friends were getting theirs done, the answer is, I don't know. Too busy with other things, I guess."

With the creep in back still blowing his horn, Jessie started the car, slipping into the first empty parking space.

"You *could*," I said again.

"Well," said Jessie, looking in the rearview mirror and tilting her head this way and that.

"I'll even let you go first."

"We'll see," she said, getting out of the car and locking the door. "We'll see."

The Earring Boutique was on the bottom floor of the mall, way down at one end, and was all glass and glitter. There were earrings everywhere, on shelves and down the walls and on spinning racks in the middle of the floor. "You think that's where they do it?" I said, pointing to a high chair in front of a sort of desk that faced a mirror lined all around with movie-star lights. "Right there?"

"I guess," Jessie said. "At least it's not crowded. You won't have to wait."

"Me? How about *we?* You said you'd see and we're here now and I'll still let you go first." I swallowed hard, hoping my voice didn't sound as shaky as it felt and trying not to look at the salesclerk with about a million earrings in each ear who was hovering in the background.

"Anything I can help you ladies with today?" she asked, coming closer.

"Well, yes," said Jessie after a pause. "The two of us would like to have our ears pierced."

With that the clerk whipped out a tray, and we were staring down at a whole collection of little round gold Jessie Barnes earrings. "This is the type we use for people just getting their ears pierced," she said. "So take your time and pick out the ones you want."

"Well, these for me," Jessie said, pointing to a pair that looked like all the rest. "And how about these slightly smaller ones for you, Livvy? They'd be perfect."

Yeah, sure, I thought. I reached into my pocket and took out the Kleenex, unfolding it and dropping the silver fish onto the counter. "Oh, that's okay," I said. "I brought my own."

The fish were brilliant. They sparkled and almost swished there on the glass. And they sort of blew everything else away.

"We can't use those," the salesclerk said. "The only ones we're allowed to use are the studs with 24-carat gold over stainless-steel posts. We have to watch out for infection."

"I think you have to be able to turn them every day till the holes heal," said Jessie, who was suddenly the world authority on ear piercing. "I thought you knew that."

"But I *never* get infections. Never in my whole life, even the time I cut my finger on the lid of the soup can and it got all red and yucky and then went away. So I'll just use these, anyway. I want the fish."

"Can't do it," the clerk said, shaking her head. "Anyway, your mother's right—you do have to turn the studs every day."

"She's not my mother!" I shouted, the words bouncing off the glass and crashing out into the mall. "Why does everybody keep thinking she's my mother when she's not. But these are my *real* mother's earrings, and if

I can't use them then I'm not getting my stupid ears pierced *ever.*" And I grabbed the fish and shoved them into my pocket.

The clerk gasped, and Jessie stepped back. I tried not to see her face, but it was reflected all around me, and I watched it go from pulled and twisted to flat as she took a deep breath and said, "If that's what you choose, Livvy, then please wait for me outside while I get my ears pierced."

I sat on a bench in the mall, facing away from the Earring Boutique, and watched a man trying on shoes in a shop across the way. I felt small and wormy and could almost hear you whispering, "Wanton words," Althea. I planned how I was never going to speak to Jessie Barnes again and wanted to tell her I was sorry, but just thinking about saying it made the words stick in my throat.

The man paid for his shoes, got his package, and left the store, and I began to think that maybe Jessie Barnes had finished, too. That maybe she had gone off and abandoned me there, on a bench in the middle of the mall. I turned around quickly just as she came to the door and called, "If you've changed your mind, Livvy, come along now. It won't take long and it really doesn't hurt."

I wanted to stay and I wanted to go. Finally *go* won out, and I got up and scuffed my way across the hall and climbed up onto the chair. I couldn't look at Jessie and I couldn't look at the clerk and I didn't want to look at myself, but there I was, staring at myself in the mirror.

"Okay," said the clerk, rubbing alcohol on my earlobes and then straightening my head with her hands and reaching for a purple marker. "First I put a dot on each ear to show where I think the earrings should go—you let me know if they're all right." I stared hard at my dotted ears and tried not to see the rest of my face, which looked all splotched and glary.

She took something like a small gun out of the drawer. "This is what I use to actually make the holes," she said, holding it up. "It makes a noise like a stapler, but it doesn't hurt, except for a small sting."

With that I closed my eyes and crossed my fingers and heard a thunk and then another thunk and felt the stings. And when I had the nerve to look, there was a gold ball in each ear, tiny, like a grain of sand. But okay.

We had lunch in the Food Hall, where it was loud and noisy, and we ate without saying anything. After a while, Jessie opened a bag of potato chips and held them out to me. "There's something I've been wanting to talk to you about, Livvy." She concentrated on the chips awhile before going on. "It's just that—well, I'm not Althea. I'll never *be* Althea. And I'm certainly not trying to take her place. I think you and I both know that." She stopped and waited until I nodded.

"And between the two of us—well, there're going to be rough spots along the way that we're going to have to work on. If you see what I'm trying to say."

"Yeah, okay," I said, looking down at the pickle curled on my plate, feeling the *I'm sorry* words still locked inside me.

On the way home, Jessie and I stopped at The Turnabout Shop to show Ivy our ears.

"They're beautiful. *You're* beautiful," she said, leading us over to the eagle mirror so we could see ourselves.

"Can we get our ears pierced, too?" asked Meg and Nell, coming forward from where they'd been playing at the back of the shop.

"Someday," said Ivy. "When you're as old as Livvy. Now show Aunt Jessie what you've been doing."

They all moved away, but I stayed where I was, in front of the mirror, opening my eyes and closing them and opening them again, thinking that maybe someday your earrings might swing and sway on me the way they did on you, Althea. What do you think?

When we got home, Jessie parked the car in back and we got out and headed for the fire escape. "Thanks for the earrings and all," I said. "And I'm sorry," I added all in a rush.

But Jessie must have heard me, because she reached out and squeezed my hand as we started up the steps.

11

Lu and I were out at recess with Lawanda, Rosie, Katie, and the rest. We were down by the fence, talking about earrings, and I had on my fish ones. As I walked in circles to show them off, they jingled and swayed and made giant shadows on the ground. Over by the door, Ms. Crivello stood ringing a bell, and ringing it, and ringing it. And then I woke and knew it was all a dream. But the bell kept ringing.

I sat up in bed and peered through the dark at my open door and felt Max against my feet. I thought of that other phone call in the middle of the night and reached for the cat, pulling him close. The ringing stopped. I heard Jessie's voice, sleepy at first, and then suddenly wide-awake, sharp and pointy. I saw the glow in the hall as she snapped on her bedside lamp.

Still holding Max, I made my way to her room, stopping just outside the door. My feet were suddenly like ice, even though the night was hot, and I had trouble catching my breath.

"What's happened?" I asked, moving into the room as she put back the phone. "Is something wrong?"

Jessie sat for a moment, still staring at the phone, before she turned to look at me. "That was my father. There's a fire at The Turnabout Shop. Some woman who lives in one of those houses across the street woke up and saw the flames and called the fire department. Then she called Ivy."

I held Max tighter, digging my fingers into his fur, until he finally wriggled loose and jumped out of my arms and ran out into the hall. "Fire?" I said.

"Yes," said Jessie, and suddenly she was off the bed, yanking clothes out of the closet and the top dresser drawer. "I've got to get over there, but I don't want to leave you here alone, so I think I'll call Lu's father and ask if I can drop you off with them."

"No," I said. "No. I want to go with you. I have to go."

"All right, then, I don't have time to argue. But get some clothes on—I need to get out of here."

I dressed as quickly as I could and followed Jessie through the kitchen.

"We should have gone the front way," said Jessie as we stumbled in the dark down the fire escape, past Nadine and Charlie's silent apartment and onto the parking area. Our feet crunched against the stones, and the noise of the engine roared into the alley so that I held my breath, half expecting lights to go on everywhere and a bunch of sleepy people to yell for us to keep quiet.

I'd never been out in the middle of the night before, and it was weird riding through streets that were almost totally deserted except for a couple of cabs and a few cars. I wanted to ask Jessie about the fire—where it had started and how bad it was—and exactly what Barney had said when he called, but her face was stiff, like a mask. And when we stopped for traffic lights, she drummed her fingers against the steering wheel and didn't say anything.

I stared out the window, and though I was pretty sure we were going the way we always did, everything seemed strange, as if I were seeing it for the first time. We went past an all-night supermarket, but even that looked forlorn and deserted; past rows of darkened houses and little shops shut tight. Then suddenly there was a glow in the sky, and when we rounded the corner we saw something out of a movie or a TV show, with a glare of lights and police cars crisscrossing the street. A policeman came up to the car, saying, "Street's closed, you'll have to detour. Back up and head west for a block and—"

"No. You don't understand. That's my shop," said Jessie. "Mine and my mother's. A neighbor called and told us and we came right over."

"Okay, then. Pull up to the curb and go on through to where those people are standing, but don't cross the yellow tape," he said, turning away before Jessie could ask him anything else.

We parked, got out, and made our way past police cars with radios squawking crazily, toward a group of people huddled together. Beyond them I could see giant firetrucks and just past those the outline of The Turnabout Shop, the front window broken and flames licking at the edges. The smell of smoke hung over everything. My eyes stung and my face felt hot, though the rest of me was shivery cold. I stopped to stamp my feet, wrapping my arms across my chest, but Jessie pushed me through the crowd as she made her way to the front.

"Oh, you poor dear. And to think of all those pretty things—just gone, like that," said a woman in a yellow bathrobe, a hairnet on her head. She caught Jessie by the arm and gave her a sort of hug. "I'm Pearl, from across the street, though like as not you don't recognize me with my hair done flat like this. It was me who called in the alarm. Me who called your mother. They got it just about under control now, but you should've seen it before—flames shooting clear up to the sky near about."

"I just can't believe it," said Jessie as we stood watching water from the hoses arching over the building.

"You should've seen it before," Pearl said again, shaking her head. "Your mother and father are over there, talking to the fire chief. Why don't you go on with them—I'll mind the girl."

"Well, thanks," said Jessie. "Okay, Livvy? You stay here and I'll be back in a few minutes."

I nodded and watched her go. Pearl caught hold of me and pulled me back a little. "Those pretty things," she said, sighing. "Those pretty things."

I closed my eyes and saw them all—the eagle mirror and Max's piano stool, the platter that looked like a lettuce leaf, rocking chairs and candlesticks. I saw the kaleidoscope, the fan, the spinning wheel. And the toys Lu and I had set up that Saturday—dolls with china heads, the alphabet blocks, the whale bank. It wasn't until I opened my eyes that I could make those things disappear.

Then I remembered the loom. Jessie's loom, which had been in the basement of The Turnabout Shop on account of me being in the loom room and which had now gone up in the fire. Like everything else. And I started to shake again.

"Fire's just about out now," said Pearl, and I wondered how long we'd been standing there like that. When I looked around, I saw that some of the people had gone, that others were turning to go.

"You know something," she said. "I could sure use some coffee about now. Why don't I run inside and make some and bring it out for your mother and your grandparents. What d'you think?"

"Okay, I guess. I'll go on over there," I said, pointing to where Jessie and Ivy and Barney were standing. And it wasn't until Pearl was gone that I realized I hadn't told her that Jessie Barnes wasn't my mother.

When I went up to them, Barney and Ivy gave me hugs and—now this is the totally weird part, Althea—Jessie Barnes put her arm around my shoulder *and* I let it stay there. We stood together, the four of us, watching the firemen as they started to put away their hoses, listening as they called back and forth to one another.

"Like I told you folks, we'll know more in a day or so, but right now it looks like the fire started from some faulty wiring in the basement of that empty place next door," the chief said, coming up to us. His face was

115

streaked with sweat, and he wiped it with his sleeve before moving off.

"I guess we should go," Ivy said. "I mean, there's no point in just standing here."

"Yes," said Jessie. But we didn't move, as if our feet were stuck to the street, or else maybe The Turnabout Shop had reached out and taken hold of us with invisible fingers.

After a while Pearl came back with a thermos of coffee, a bunch of Styrofoam cups, and a Coke for me, and sort of shuffled us across the street. She settled us into bouncy metal chairs lined in front of her house and pulled a package of cookies out of her bathrobe pocket. "Now the thing to do, once you're done here," she said, "is to go on home and get some rest. If you ask my opinion, things always look better in the morning."

I watched the daylight edging onto the sky, took a gulp of my Coke, felt it fizzle at the back of my nose, and thought how no matter what, I was pretty sure things at The Turnabout Shop weren't going to look any better tomorrow. Which was really today.

12

I must have slept, although when we got home and Jessie told me just to stretch out on the bed for a while, I told her I never would. Sleep, I mean. But when I woke, the sun was pouring into my room and I felt hot and sticky and was still in the clothes I had thrown on in the middle of the night. My mouth tasted gross from Coke and cookies and not brushing my teeth afterward, and I lay there for a while, staring at the girl in the rabbit picture and trying to pretend that everything that had happened hadn't. Except I knew it had.

When I heard voices coming from the kitchen, I got up to see who was there and found Jessie having coffee with Miss Winston and Celie.

"Here she is," Miss Winston said, holding out her

hand to me and pulling me toward an empty chair. "We were just telling Jessie how very sorry we are. And I had this coffee cake just coming out of the oven, so I thought I'd bring it along."

I guess I looked sort of blank, because as Jessie was getting me a plate and a glass of milk, she explained. "I couldn't get to sleep, so as soon as it was good and light, I went out for a long walk, and when I got back Robert was working on the front door, so I stopped to tell him about the fire."

"And Robert told me," Miss Winston put in.

"And when I came in from my jog, Miss Winston told *me*," said Celie.

"And I just gathered up the coffee cake and here we are. What a shame, what a shame." She sighed deeply, and I could tell by the way she said it that Miss Winston had probably said What a shame a bunch of times already.

"I guess it's too early to tell what your plans are," said Celie, pinching a raisin off the edge of the plate.

"That's what I was trying to figure out on my walk this morning," Jessie said. "Part of me thinks that I never want to see another antique, or another shop. And the other part—" She stopped and shrugged. "But as you say, it's still too early. What I want to do, though, once we've gotten cleaned up, is go on over there and see how things look in the daytime."

"Now we'll just run along and let you tend to things," Miss Winston said, hopping up.

"Oh no, I didn't mean that," said Jessie. "We're not in any rush."

"I know, I know, but I'm sure you're anxious and anyway, I left without half telling Dudley where I was going."

"Just promise to let us know if there's anything we can do," said Celie, taking her mug to the sink and washing it."

"Goodbye."

"Goodbye."

"And thanks for coming," called Jessie as we stood in the doorway and watched one go down and the other go up the stairs.

I took my shower first, and when Jessie came out from taking hers, I was standing in the kitchen, using the door of the microwave as a mirror and dabbing alcohol on my ears and carefully turning my earrings, the way the clerk in the Earring Boutique had told us to. "Don't forget your ears," I said.

"My ears?" said Jessie, crinkling her brow and looking at me as if everything that had happened before the fire was about a million years ago. She laughed. "You're right," she said. "The last thing we need now is an infected ear." And she reached for the alcohol.

While she was getting dressed, I talked to Max about what had happened last night, mostly the part about Pearl serving Coke and coffee in the middle of the night. I guess I couldn't bear to remember the rest. Anyway, when Jessie was ready, we went down the fire escape and found Charlie and Nadine waiting for us.

"Robert told us about the fire, and we just wanted you both to know how sorry we are," said Nadine.

"And if you're on your way over there, we're going with you," said Charlie, who for once had on shoes instead of roller blades. "Come on, we'll all go in our car."

"You don't have to. We'll be okay," said Jessie, but suddenly her voice sounded quivery and not okay at all. "Besides, I need my car. Livvy and I are going to my mother's afterward."

"We'll follow you, then," said Nadine. "Just lead the way."

And when we parked the cars and got out a block from where The Turnabout Shop used to be, I think Jessie was glad to have them. I know I was.

Everything was Sunday-morning quiet, but eerier, especially when a church bell from somewhere in the distance started to ring. A few neighbors stood on the sidewalk and we went toward them in slow motion, stopping to look at the blackened bricks out front and then inching closer, peering into the skeleton of the building. There were pools of water on the ground, and the air was still heavy with the smell of smoke.

"Holy cow," said Charlie.

"It's even worse than I imagined," whispered Nadine.

I pulled back and went to stand in a patch of sunlight, feeling that same cold shiver from the night before starting up.

Jessie walked over to a fireman and came back carrying a round piece of charred wood. "He found this," she said, holding it up.

"From the spinning wheel," I said after staring at it for a while. I reached out to touch it and it felt clammy and damp and I pulled my finger away. "What's the fireman doing here, anyway?"

"Making sure nothing's still smoldering, before they let the landlord send someone in to board the place up," said Jessie. "Come on, let's go. There's nothing for us to do here."

When we got to Ivy and Barney's, they were having lunch. Jessie made us sandwiches, and we sat down with them on the back porch. When we were finishing, Paul and Gloria came in with Noah and Susie, and the rest of us told them more about the fire. Sometime later, Meaghan and Bill and Paulie came, and a little bit after that, Susan and Bob and Meg and Nell. And each time someone arrived, we started over and told the story from the beginning.

We spent most of the afternoon talking about The Turnabout Shop. About the day it opened and how there were balloons out front tied to the back of a rocking chair, how the first-ever customer was a woman with about a million rings who bought something called a jardiniere and came back the next day for an old wooden cradle because she wanted to put magazines in it. Barney brought out a yellow-looking newspaper article about the shop, and Ivy found a bunch of pictures—of opening day, and one of Noah and Susie standing out front when they were really little, and even one of Max on his piano stool, before he was Max and came to live with Jessie and me.

Meanwhile, I watched Jessie Barnes, the way she was stroking the stack of pictures, running her fingers over the newspaper article. I watched the others, too—Ivy and Barney, Meaghan and Paul, Noah, Susie, and the rest, thinking how they made me feel that it was okay for me to be there. Better than okay. Only, the whole time I was thinking this, I was half holding my breath.

Waiting.

For somebody to remember Jessie's loom and that it was really important to her and that if I hadn't come to stay with her it'd still be back at the apartment and not in the basement of The Turnabout Shop. Not lost in the fire.

That maybe it was partly my fault.

And that maybe they wouldn't want me here anymore.

Just one thing, though, Althea. The way I figure it, if it's partly my fault (about Jessie's loom), then it's partly yours, too. For telling Fred the lawyer to send me to her in the first place. I really need to talk to you about this. I really need someone to help me sort it out.

Do you hear what I'm saying, Althea? Are you listening to me?

Nobody mentioned the loom, though, and after we'd been sitting there for a long time, and Noah was kicking at the slats on the porch rail and I was cracking my knuckles and Susie and Nell and Meg were all three fighting over the same chair, Gloria said why didn't we go somewhere. Noah found a ball in the cupboard under the stairs, and we went out back and played soccer till we were hot and sweaty. Then we switched to croquet, except that Paulie kept being a pain and running off with the balls, so we gave up and went inside and watched a movie.

It got to be suppertime, but when nobody seemed ready to leave, Meaghan and Susan made salad and Paul and Barney went out for a ton of pizza. Susie and Meg and I set the table in the dining room, and we all sat down to eat. For a while the grown-ups tried to talk about the Orioles and how maybe they could win the pennant if they kept going the way they were now, about Barney's roses and whether it would storm later. But no matter what, they always came back to the fire at The Turnabout Shop.

After supper, when the dishes were done, we all sat on the porch for a while and watched the fireflies, until Paulie turned into a crank and started to whine and then to cry. That's when everybody decided it was time to go home.

All the talking and just being there had helped, though, if you want my opinion. I could tell by the way Jessie's hands weren't clenched tight on the steering wheel as we headed home, and by the way the flat line of her mouth went a little bit up at the corners. Not a smile, but up anyway.

As for me, I crammed the loom into the far back corner of my mind and hoped that it would stay there.

13

In the days right after the fire, Jessie and Ivy were busy in the office on Ivy's third floor doing what they called paperwork and making a list for the insurance company of everything that had burned. There was even a picture inventory of most of the furniture and dishes and stuff that had been in the shop. Just flipping through the folder made me feel sad all over again.

I kept going to my art classes and my swimming lessons and went from being a minnow to a red snapper and was pretty sure I'd be a shark sometime soon, because one day my teacher said I took to swimming like a fish to water. Then she laughed and slapped the side of her leg and told me to swim across the pool and back.

I still hung out with Lu and went with her to her

aunt's a couple of times. Once her aunt took us to the aquarium, which was really cool.

One thing I'm not sure about, Althea, but did I ever tell you what Lu looks like? She's the same height and sort of shape as me, except she has this short, really curly hair, and when I told her once I'd trade her, she said not to say that till after I'd seen her in the middle of a humid Baltimore summer, when her hair got even shorter and curlier and looked like a Brillo pad. I've seen her that way now, and I'd *still* trade if I could. Since I can't, I sometimes wear my hair pulled back in a ponytail to keep cool—and so my earrings will show. Not *your* earrings. Not yet. I'm saving them till I'm older, like maybe thirteen.

At home Jessie read the "Help Wanted" columns in the newspaper and talked on the phone to people about job opportunities and looked into what she'd need to be certified as a teacher. "I don't think I can go through it all again," she said one night after supper. We were sitting on the fire escape, watching a boy kicking a tin can down the alley. "With the shop and all." She stopped for a while, concentrating hard on the boy and the can, as if that was all that mattered.

"I didn't want a shop, not at first, anyway. I always saw myself as a teacher, making my favorite parts of history come alive for middle-school kids year after year. Which

I know sounds incredibly hokey, but I was sure I could pull it off. Only there I was, spending every spare minute prowling Antique Row and going to sales and auctions. And then one day Ivy suggested we open a shop and we did. And I couldn't believe that every day I was getting to do what I liked best in the whole world."

Jessie waited a minute before going on. "But now—with what happened—I just don't think—"

She stopped, and I didn't know what to say. So after a while I did the only thing I could think to do, which was go inside and fix two bowls of chocolate-chip–cookie-dough frozen yogurt and bring them outside, along with the book Barney had given me.

We ate the yogurt and then, by the light from the kitchen door, I read *Millions of Cats* out loud as the darkness settled down around us.

One day, Barney, who is a judge and was taking a week's vacation, picked me up after swimming, and on the way back to his house he took a detour, right into the neighborhood where The Turnabout Shop used to be. A couple of blocks down the avenue, he pulled up in front of a vacant building with a gigantic window across the front with RED BALLOON CAFÉ painted on it. Under that was a FOR RENT sign.

"The Red Balloon never got off the ground, and the

place closed," Barney said as we got out of the car and walked across the sidewalk. "So what do you think?"

I looked at him and at the Red Balloon Café, and all of a sudden a lightbulb went on in my head, just the way it does in cartoons and comic strips. "For The Turnabout Shop, you mean. For The Turnabout Shop. Yes, but do you think—I mean—"

"It'll be a tough sell," said Barney. "For both of us."

"On account of Jessie?"

"Pretty much. I think Ivy'd be willing to try again, but she'd never push Jess into another shop if that's not what she wants."

"But she *does* want it. She *has* to want it, because of the way she cared about the things in the shop and where they came from and who used to own them a long time ago. Except," I said, slowing down, "she's been reading the Help Wanted ads and talking to people about jobs and all."

"I know, I know," said Barney, taking a notebook out of his pocket and writing down the phone number on the FOR RENT sign.

While he did that, I moved closer, pressing my forehead against the plate-glass window and peering into the shadowy insides of the store.

We got back in the car and went to Ivy and Barney's house, because Jessie was meeting a friend for lunch and

I was staying at the house till she came to get me. The whole time we were eating, I waited for Barney to say something about the empty Red Balloon Café, but he never did. And afterward, when we were finished, he went out to work on his garden, and Ivy and I sat on the porch and read *Caddie Woodlawn* to each other, because she remembered reading it when she was young and wanted to see if she still liked it. She did.

Jessie came back, and Barney brought out glasses of iced tea, and for a while we sat talking about nothing much.

"Well, Livvy, we'd better be on our way. I want to stop at the Giant Store on the way home." Jessie reached for her purse and started to get up.

I looked at Barney and Barney looked at me. "Now wait a minute, Jess," he said. "Let me tell you what I saw today on the way home from picking Livvy up."

All of a sudden I couldn't wait anymore, and the words were spilling out of my mouth. "We went by this store and then we stopped and got out and it used to be the Red Balloon Café and Barney said it never got off the ground and now it's empty and it's for rent and we looked in the window, which is enormous and goes all across the front, and it'd make a perfect Turnabout Shop."

Ivy gasped, and Jessie made a wrinkly face and let out

a terrible sigh. "I don't think I could ever take on another shop again," she said. "Not after losing one. It's just too risky."

"But you *have* to," I cried out. "You *have* to. On account of you have to be a survivor—the way Althea said. You can't just stop. You can't just give up." I felt stinging tears in my eyes and turned my face away.

"The child's right, you know," said Ivy.

"It really wouldn't hurt to go and look at it," said Barney. "I jotted down the number of the rental agent."

Just then the phone rang, and Ivy went inside to answer it. Barney spotted the mailman and headed out to meet him. It was Jessie Barnes and me—and Cider sleeping under the swing.

"Is it because of the loom?" I said. "Because of the loom that you don't want another shop?"

"The loom? No, not the loom. It's everything being lost, and all the time, all the work. Why would you ask about the loom?"

"Because Susie and Noah said my room used to be the loom room, and then by the time I got here the loom was in the basement of The Turnabout Shop, and then the fire happened and the loom burned and it was maybe my fault—"

I got up and went over to the rail and stood looking

out, only the trees and bushes and even Barney and the mailman were all blurry, and tears rolled down my face.

"Livvy, Livvy," said Jessie Barnes, coming to stand behind me, putting her hands on my shoulders, turning me around. "It's not your fault. Not the fire, or the loom being lost, or anything."

"But it was important to you. The loom, I mean, and if I hadn't—"

"Sure it was important, but you're more important than a dozen looms, two dozen looms." She pulled me close in a hug that wasn't exactly a hug, only it felt okay. "Besides, I like having you here. You're more fun than a loom any day. You laugh at my jokes, such as they are, and watch videos with me and make me popcorn at night, and bowls of frozen yogurt. We go to lunch together, and—and you talked me into getting my ears pierced after all these years."

She stepped back, still holding tight to my shoulders. "You—you're—oh, you know what I'm trying to say."

"What Charlie says? That looms are looms but kids are cool?" I said.

"Wise man, that Charlie," said Jessie Barnes, giving me another one of her funky hugs before sitting down.

Ivy came out from inside, and Barney brought the mail and dropped it on the table. Jessie picked up her glass and put it down again. "I don't know," she said, shaking her head. "I'm not making any promises, but maybe we could go by and look at it sometime."

We did. The very next day, because, as Barney said, "We can't let any grass grow under anyone's feet." Lu went with us, and as we pulled up in front of the Red Balloon Café, we saw Ivy and Barney and a woman I figured was from the real-estate office standing on the sidewalk.

"This is a wonderful property," the woman, whose name was Carol, said after Barney had introduced us all. She unlocked the door and propped it open. "In case it's a little stuffy inside," she added, ushering us in.

The air was warm and smelled of spices, maybe from long-ago dinners. There were red balloons painted on the walls, and tables pushed off to the side, with chairs piled on top. Lu and I took off, our flip-flops slapping against the floor as we circled the big front room. We went through one swinging door to what used to be the kitchen and out another. We sat on the window seat that ran across the front and hurried off to explore an alcove to the side of the front door.

"You could put the toys here," I said, blinking at the games and blocks and dolls and tops I could almost see jumbled there.

"And there's even a shelf for the little dishes," said Lu.

"The overall space is wonderful," said Ivy, "though the balloons would have to go."

"The room in back that was the kitchen would make a terrific office," said Barney.

"And the basement's absolutely dry and great for storage," said Carol, unlocking another door and leading us down the steps. Jessie trailed after us, never opening her mouth, even while Barney checked out the furnace and Ivy commented on the shelves running around the walls.

Back upstairs, Jessie sat on the window seat, looking all around, while Lu and I went back to the toy alcove and Ivy and Barney talked to Carol about measurements.

Say something, I wanted to shout at Jessie. Don't just *sit* there—*say something.*

Finally she got up and moved to the rear of the store. "You know," she said, "this back wall would be perfect for hanging quilts on. And if we had several, we could keep rotating them."

Everyone was suddenly quiet, and we could hear the cars outside on the street. Barney cleared his throat, and when I looked at him, he winked.

14

It's the middle of August now, and a whole lot has happened since our day at the Red Balloon Café, which is going to be The Turnabout Shop. There are carpenters working on what used to be the kitchen, and a painter is painting the walls in the big front room an incredible pale pink. "To pick up the highlights in the furniture," Jessie says.

Ivy and Jessie have been making lists of chairs and tables and clocks and glass-fronted bookcases they want for the shop, and going to sales and bringing everything they find back to store on Ivy and Barney's third floor, crowding it all into Ivy's office and the room that used to be Paul's when he was little. Until the work in the shop is finished.

Tomorrow Jessie and Susie and I are heading down to the Eastern Shore to go to an antiques auction. We'll stay overnight in a motel, and then we'll meet the rest of the family in Bethany for our week at the beach.

I'm excited about the beach, but in a weird way I'm excited about the auction, too. I already have a list in my head of the things I hope we'll find for the new shop—a spinning wheel, a quilt for Jessie's wall, old-time toys, maybe even a mirror with an eagle on the top.

They'll each have a story to tell. Same as I do. About you, Althea, and how I wish you were here. About Lu and Charlie and the others. About Ivy and Barney, the aunts, the uncles, the cousins.

And about Jessie Barnes and me.